Nora, Nora

In the 1960s Lytton, an insular small town in America's Deep South, offers few chances for a bright young twelve-year-old like Peyton McKenzie to spread her wings.

Not, that is, until Peyton's cousin Nora drives into town in a bright pink Thunderbird. The red-haired, fiercely independent Nora freely speaks her views on everything, shocking the narrow-minded townsfolk to their core.

To Peyton, she is a breath of fresh air.

Nora, Nora

SELECT EDITIONS

This condensation has been created by The Reader's Digest Association Limited by special arrangement with Little, Brown and Company (UK).

The original edition of this book was published and copyrighted as follows: NORA, NORA, published at £17.99 by Little, Brown, © 2000 by Anne Rivers Siddons. The right of Anne Rivers Siddons to be identified as the author of this work has been asserted by her in accordance with the Copyright, Designs and Patents Act 1988. Cover illustration and front cover/spine of slipcase: watercolour by Tom Nachreiner. Author photo on page 135: © Jerry Bauer. Slipcase photomontage by Shark Attack.

The Reader's Digest Association Limited,
11 Westferry Circus, Canary Wharf, London E14 4HE.

www.readersdigest.co.uk
ISBN 0 276 42555 3

Printed and bound by GGP Media, Pössneck, Germany

Nora, Nora

Anne Rivers Siddons

READER'S DIGEST SELECT EDITIONS
CONDENSED BOOKS DIVISION

PROLOGUE

The Losers Club met every weekday afternoon at four o'clock in the toolshed behind the Methodist parsonage on the corner of Peyton McKenzie's street. Peyton would be out of her seventh-grade classes at the Lytton Grammar School and sometimes through her homework by then; her father would be cloistered away in his study; and Clothilde would be moving ponderously about the kitchen preparing supper for them. Peyton would have shed her school clothes and skimmed gratefully into her jeans and a T-shirt, looking like a starved pullet, all air-light bones and translucent razor angles.

Ernie Longworth, the second member of the club after Peyton, would be dressed in the bursting coveralls he wore all day in the pursuit of his duties as sexton of the Methodist church. Ernie was thirty-four years old, very fat and pale and fish-eyed behind his thick glasses, and sullen and rude to almost everyone but the members of the Losers Club and his darting tarantula mother, the parsonage housekeeper, with whom he lived in a little house behind the minister's official residence. He read voraciously, and fiercely loved classical music.

Ernie had been Peyton's friend ever since she was old enough to toddle up the street alone and discover him pottering around his lair, a meticulously kept corner of the toolshed that held a book-case, a gut-springing easy chair, a tape-mended ottoman and a black pot-bellied stove. Ernie kept a small white plastic Philco radio on a shelf there, and there were usually three Coca-Colas in an old red metal ice chest, waiting for the club members when they congregated. Though Ernie treated Peyton as an equal, talking to her as if she were his age, he was generally so waspishly ineffectual that no one, including Peyton, took him seriously. But she was still proud to have him in the Losers Club, because of his obviously superior mind and opinions on cultural matters, and she often parroted these to Clothilde, who only snorted.

'What good they do him if he can't get himself no further than that ol' toolshed and his mama's supper table,' she would say.

'He *wants* to do what he does,' Peyton would say. 'It leaves him more time for cultivating the mind than a real job in Atlanta would do. Ernie cares more for things of the spirit than of the flesh.'

'Look to me like he care plenty about his flesh,' Clothilde said, but she said it good-naturedly. The McKenzies' housekeeper did not see anything amiss with the time Peyton spent in the parsonage toolshed with Ernie Longworth. Everyone knew Ernie was harmless, if strange. Everyone knew that Peyton McKenzie was nothing but a thin, frail, 'nervous' child; the Peytons, her long-dead mother's family, had always been aristocratically nervous and frail. Lila Lee Peyton had, indeed, died of that frailty at Peyton's birth.

Clothilde—or Chloe—did not even mind that her own grandson, eight-year-old Boot, was the third member of the Losers Club. Almost dwarfishly small for his age, Boot had been born with a clubfoot. Chloe had been bringing him to work with her ever since he was two, when his own mother vanished into the haze of neon light that was Atlanta. She was grateful that he had a place to go in the afternoons for a couple of hours, so that she could prepare the McKenzie supper in peace.

Boot was always the last one to appear at Losers Club meetings, because his infirmity slowed him down, and the toolshed lay at the far end of the parsonage garden. This was an overgrown jungle of crazed rosebushes, rampaging wisteria, and kudzu-shrouded cement benches and plaster statuary. Boot had a hard time threading his way through this virulent green maze; they could hear his floundering in the undergrowth and the clump-scrape of his heavy leather boot on the gravel path long before his cheerful face appeared in the doorway. It gave them time to change the subject if they had been talking about him, or about some topic that might be offensive to him. In Lytton, Georgia, in 1961, there were many of those, and no one else in the town, black or white, thought to spare the tender sensibilities of a clubfooted little Negro boy. Wise, pragmatic Boot did not mind. He appreciated the gesture of the stopped conversations and always pretended that he had not the faintest idea what they had been talking about.

'Awright,' he would pipe, heaving himself down on the ottoman, 'Who done the dumbest thing today?'

1

Peyton McKenzie changed her name when she was six years old. All her life she had been called Prilla or sometimes Priscilla, her first name, but that stopped with rocklike finality when the first scabby classmate at elementary school began to chant, 'Prilla, Prilla, mother-killer.' By the time the entire first grade in the Lytton Grammar School had taken up the refrain, Peyton McKenzie had been born.

'It's a man's name, for heaven's sake,' her Aunt Augusta had said in exasperation. 'What's wrong with "Priscilla"? It's a lovely name.'

'Peyton is my middle name,' Peyton had muttered. 'It's as much mine as Priscilla.' Both she and Augusta McKenzie knew there would be no changing of Peyton's mind, but Augusta saw it as her duty, as the dominant woman in Peyton's life, to do battle with the granite streak of wilfulness in her niece. On the death of Peyton's mother, Frazier McKenzie had placed the day-to-day shaping of his daughter in his sister-in-law's hands. By the time of Peyton's first great rebellion, aunt and niece were old adversaries. Augusta McKenzie knew full well she wasn't going to win this one. But she would never know why, because Peyton never told anyone about the cold, whining little chant at school that morning, not until much later. Her beleaguered teacher soon forgot about the name change entirely.

Only Peyton remembered, each day of her life and deep in her smallest cell, that she had, indeed, killed her mother. If her father never so much as hinted to her that he held her responsible for the extinguishing of the radiant flame her mother had been, Peyton put it down to Frazier McKenzie's natural reticence. He had been, all her life, as politely remote as a benign godparent. He was so with everyone, except Peyton's older brother, Buddy. When Buddy died in an accident in his air-force trainer, when Peyton was five, Frazier McKenzie closed up shop on his laughter, anger, small foolishnesses, and large passions. Now, at twelve, Peyton could remember no other father than the cooled and static one she had. Her father seemed to remember her only intermittently.

She told the Losers Club about the name change on a February day when it seemed as if earth and sky were made of the same grey sodden cloth. It happens sometimes in the Deep South when winter can no longer muster an honest cold but will not admit the warm tides of spring lapping at the gates. It is a climatic sulk, and can last for weeks, exhausting spirits and fraying nerves. Ernie had been so petulant that Boot had told him to shut up if he didn't have anything to add to the day's litanies of abasement. Even Boot seemed more dutiful than enthusiastic over his contribution to the club's itinerary, a lustreless account of wiping out the Canaday children's hopscotch grid with his orthotic boot.

'Well, if I couldn't do better than that, I just wouldn't say anything,' Ernie sniffed.

'You *ain't* said anything,' Boot pointed out. 'And I jes' as soon you didn't. You as mean as an old settin' hen today. Peyton gon' have to come up with something really fine to make up for you.'

Two pairs of cool eyes turned towards Peyton.

'I killed my mother,' she said, her heart beating hard with the sheer daring of it, and the first opening of the pit of that old pain. The others were silent, looking at her.

'You ain't, neither,' Boot said finally.

'You flatter yourself,' Ernie said.

But they knew they were bested by a long shot.

'I did, too,' Peyton said. 'She died not a day after I was born. She bled to death. Everybody knows that. I've always known it.'

'Then why didn't you say?' Boot asked.

'You'd have only said I was showing off. Not only did I kill her, but when I was in first grade I changed my name to Peyton because the kids were singing a song about "Prilla, Prilla, mother-killer".'

She folded her arms over her thin chest complacently.

Ernie leaned back in his armchair and picked up his copy of *The Inferno*. 'Meeting adjourned,' he said coldly.

They watched him for a couple of minutes, but he did not look up, and finally Boot said, 'Come on, Peyton. He just mad because you outdone him. Let's go to your house.'

At the edge of the sidewalk in front of Peyton's house, he looked up at her. 'You really kill your ma?'

'I really did,' Peyton said.

THAT EVENING her father's sister-in-law, Augusta Tatum McKenzie, came for supper, bringing white rolls from the A&P grocery store. Peyton knew this made Chloe furious; she prided herself on her light, melting biscuits and rolls. But Augusta had pronounced that they were made from lard, which was very unhealthy, as well as being common.

'Where's Charles?' Frazier McKenzie asked, taking the box of rolls from her. 'Thanks, Augusta. These look very good.'

'Charles has gone fox-hunting with that lowlife Floyd Fletcher,' Augusta snapped. 'No matter that it's out of season. If Floyd weren't chief of police Charles would have been in jail long since. Sorry, that's all Floyd is. Sorry as a yard dog.'

'It's good for a man to get out in the woods sometimes,' Frazier said. 'I ought to do it more often.'

'You're too busy to hunt, Frazier,' Aunt Augusta said. She used a different voice with Peyton's father than with anyone else. 'It's been a long time since you've had time to fool around in the woods with Floyd Fletcher and that poolroom crowd. You've given up a lot for the law and your family. At least one of us knows it.'

Peyton stared at her aunt. She could not recall a single time when her father had gone off into the woods to slay foxes.

'I don't see how you can give up something you never did anyway,' she said. Her aunt brought out the mulish worst in Peyton. In her presence, Peyton turned into just what Augusta thought she was: a tall, shrinking, sulking, ungrateful preadolescent badly in need of a firm, womanly hand.

'There are a lot of things about your father you don't see,' Augusta said. 'You're old enough now to think about some of the sacrifices he's made for you, to say thank you once in a blue moon.'

Peyton got up and slammed rudely out of the breakfast room and into the kitchen, where Clothilde was whipping cream for strawberry shortcake. Chloe only looked up at her, but Peyton could feel the warm surge of her sympathy. Then she heard her father say, 'She says thank you often enough, Augusta. She's not an adult, after all. All that will come later.'

'You think?' Augusta replied relentlessly. 'Have you looked at her lately? She's taller than her mother already, taller than me. She's getting hair on her arms and legs. It's time she shaved her legs, but who is there to teach her how? And I'd get that hair cut and curled in a jiffy. You remember Lila Lee's hair, so lovely . . . I wish you'd let me take her in hand, Frazier. She'll never have any friends, boys or girls, unless we do something about that attitude. The only people she sees are that awful Ernie and that poor little Negro boy.'

Her father did not reply. Peyton stood silently, looking at Chloe, and could not get her breath.

I will not grow up, she thought. Not with her on my neck. I'll run away first. But she knew that she wouldn't. Peyton had never even taken a Greyhound bus into Atlanta alone.

She knew, too, that in a terrible way her aunt was right. She would never join the crowd of twittering, lipsticked girls and jostling, large-handed boys at the soda fountain after school. Yet each new inch of height brought her closer to a forced exit from the Losers Club. Augusta would see to that. Peyton would be isolated from the only confidants she had, the only living souls to whom she could say anything peevish and perverse that she pleased.

She stood on a frail bridge between childhood and womanhood and stared into an abyss.

'TELL ME ABOUT my mother,' she said to Chloe the next morning. It was Saturday, but Frazier McKenzie had already gone to his office above the garage and Peyton was heavy with the shapeless hours ahead of her. There was no Losers Club on Saturday.

'I done told you about your mama a million times,' Chloe said softly.

'Well, tell me again. Tell me what she looked like. Tell me what made her laugh.'

Chloe slipped eggs and bacon in front of her. 'Eat that,' she said. 'Eggs give you breasts.'

'I'd rather eat dog food,' Peyton said, near tears.

'Well, that's easy enough to get,' Chloe said. She did not push the eggs. She sensed, though she could not have articulated it, that Peyton was going to need her childhood for a long time yet.

'So, she looked like . . . what?'

'Well, she was real pretty,' Chloe said. 'She was little and slim, and light on her feet. She had hair that kind of spun around her head, real fine and blondelike, and curly. She never had to go to no beauty shop. She used to sing and dance around the house even when by herself, and she and your daddy and Buddy used to act silly all the time and play games. She was real popular; she went out all the time, to lunch at the country club, or to Atlanta to shop, or to play tennis at the club. She was gone 'most every afternoon.'

'I'm not like her at all, am I?' Peyton said in a small voice. She knew that she was not, but it was as if she had to hear it regularly lest she start to imagine a relationship that could not have been, and then feel the loss of it in her deepest heart.

Peyton had not known her grandparents George and Priscilla Peyton, but she knew about them. They were aristocrats, people who got for themselves a dazzling dryad of a daughter, people who gave her to Peyton's father, along with the gift of this great old house in Lytton, with thinly disguised apprehension.

Peyton could imagine why. Her father's family were Scots who had backed the wrong horse at the Battle of Culloden and then departed hastily for America, with nothing but their flinty reserve and the fireshot passions just beneath it that smouldered like burning peat, and their own private mythology, dark with stunted gods of water and mountain. Time, however, had mellowed the passions out of the McKenzies, so that they were now respectably Presbyterian. Peyton would not have known the dark Hebridean side of her family if it had not been for her paternal grandmother, Agnes MacLaren McKenzie.

Nana McKenzie was a throwback, a raven among the pale, fluttering female birds of Lytton. She lived alone now, since Peyton's grandfather had died ten years before, in a farmhouse at the edge of town. Nana walked into town when she wanted something, spurning her son's offers to drive her and his invitations to come and live with them in the big house.

'Surely you know that wouldn't do,' Augusta had said to Frazier when he proposed it. 'It would be a terrible influence on Peyton. Your mother's half crazy, and the whole town knows it. She makes a commotion every time she comes to town with her prophecies. We all know it's just hokum, but Ed Carruthers at the hardware store said his Negro boys have started carrying charms, to warn off the evil eye or some such nonsense. She stood in the middle of Monument Square the other day yelling "Go tell the Devil!" at a flock of crows.'

'She's not crazy, you know, Augusta,' Frazier had said tightly. 'The things she says and does have come down a thousand years in the Highlands. They make sense to her and to me, too, though I wish she wouldn't do them in the middle of town. When I was little I thought she had the Sight. She still says she does.'

He had looked levelly at Augusta, who fell silent, then turned to Peyton, who was doing her homework at the breakfast table nearby, and winked. Peyton's heart had soared. She loved her Nana McKenzie without boundary, believed with her whole heart that the old woman had the Sight, and was so warmed and energised by the wink that she said, 'Everybody knows that crows watch all week to see what sins we've committed, and on Friday they go down to hell and tell the Devil. Jaybirds do it, too. Haven't you heard of Jaybird Friday?'

'I have not, except among the Negroes,' Aunt Augusta had said. 'It's a Negro superstition, Peyton, not a Scottish one.'

'They've got crows in Scotland, too,' Peyton said rudely, and she knew at once that she had cranked it one ratchet too far.

'If I hear of Mama McKenzie creating one more scene in public I am going to speak to Floyd Fletcher,' her aunt said. 'This can't continue, Frazier.'

'I don't want to hear of your doing that, Augusta,' her father said, in a voice as austere as his profile. 'It is not your place. She is your mother-in-law, you know. She's Charlie's mother.'

'And he has not invited her into his home for more than a year now. Did you ever wonder why?'

Frazier McKenzie had turned his head slowly and looked at his sister-in-law. The sea-grey of his eyes turned to ice and his thin mouth thinned even further. 'That is enough, Augusta.'

Aunt Augusta had dropped her eyes. Soon after, she had gathered up her shopping bags and gone home. Peyton had felt exultation at her aunt's virtual banishment.

'Nana thinks I'm going to have the Sight when I'm older,' Peyton said now to Clothilde.

Chloe put down her iron and looked at her. 'I like your grandmother,' she said, 'and I believe it when she say she see stuff. But it ain't what you ought to be doing right now in your life. Look at you: you don't talk about much but your mama and your brother and you don't see many people but your grandmother and that Ernie and my own po' little Boot . . . Maybe you ought to spend some time with folks your age.'

Peyton shrugged, and went upstairs and put on her blue jeans. Then she climbed the dogwood tree at the side of the house to the tree house where she spent a great deal of time, and she opened her book. She had just discovered *The Catcher in the Rye*, and felt that somehow this book was going to change her life.

THAT NIGHT AFTER SUPPER, after her father went out to his office to polish up the Sunday-school lesson he would teach the next morning at the First Methodist Church, Peyton went into her room behind the cavernous downstairs bathroom and pulled the old projector out of her closet and hung a white sheet on the door.

She had volunteered to learn to use the old school projector when she was in the fourth grade. She proved to be deft with the wheezing old machine, and for the past three years had been the one excused from her classes to thread up and show films on the agriculture of the Urals and the Battle of Agincourt and, at Christmas, *A Christmas Carol.*

By now Peyton could have set up and operated the projector in her sleep, and in fact often did do so in the dark, when her father thought she was sleeping. She had found the projector and the cans of film one day when she was poking around in the spider room, a forbidden cubicle at the back of the garage where her father had once seen a black widow spider. She had asked him about them that night, and he had said that they were old home movies. 'You know. Things around town. This house. The church, and Nana's farm. Nana and Grandpa.'

'And us? Are we there?'

'Well . . . there are a few of your mother and your brother and me. Some birthdays and Christmases and things . . .'

'And me? Are there any of me?' Peyton asked.

'Well, you weren't born yet. About that time I moved my office out to the garage and the movie stuff got put away and I just forgot about it. What were you doing in the spider room, anyway?'

'Just looking,' Peyton mumbled, warm salt stinging her eyes. She knew that the reason her father had never made movies of her was that the pale little life that had taken his wife was nothing to be recorded. But after that the movies drew her like a magnet and it was the next week that she volunteered to be projectionist at school. After two or three weeks of practice, she went out to the garage while Frazier was in Atlanta, and moved the projector and the film into her room. She kept the projector behind her raincoat in the closet, and the round, flat cans of film under her bed. Twice a week she lay in the dark and watched a world without her whirr and flicker against her wall.

First she would put on the footage of Lytton and study the flickering images of her home town. The post office and the dry cleaner's, then the rest of the small businesses and services that made up Lytton's Main Street—a tiny grocery, a hardware store, a barbershop, a butcher shop, a lunchroom with a poolroom at the back, and a drugstore with a black marble soda fountain. Then came a ten-cent store, the Lytton Banking Company, another attorney's office, the town municipal offices, and the solitary wooden movie theatre.

Because very little in Lytton had changed appreciably since the middle thirties, the Lytton of Peyton's time was the Lytton of her family's time, too, and that soothed her. When she thought about Lytton, Georgia, it was a town of erratic sepia images bathed in silence. Peyton's reel world was also her real one.

When she had reassured herself that the town in the films was still as it had been the last time she looked, she let herself follow the camera down the side streets, where people actually lived. In one of these sequences Peyton saw her own house, looking almost precisely as it did now except for the striped awnings over the front porch that had been there then. She saw her mother, Lila Lee Peyton McKenzie, waving from the front door and doing a pantomime of a movie star being photographed. As always, when she reached this spot in the film, Peyton felt a relief so profound it almost brought her to tears. Once again she had travelled the road home and come safely to this place where her mother smiled and held out her arms in welcome. It did not matter to Peyton that the welcome was not for her. In the films and in her mind, it was always a sweet sepia summer, and time stopped on the walkway to her house, and she was home.

Once she was safe, it was easy for Peyton to watch the other films. Most of them were, she knew, made by her father because they were of her mother, so young and light-struck and beautiful that she seemed to shimmer with colour even though there was none on the film. Her mother, small and slender, her blonde hair a nimbus around her little cat's face, dancing to unheard music on the porch; her mother vamping for the camera in the back yard, where a barbecue was going on; her mother standing at the net at the little Lytton Country Club holding a tennis racket and smiling up at a tall, trim young man in tennis whites who had raised both hands and clasped them over his head in victory. He was dark and, Peyton thought, brooding and romantic-looking, as she imagined Heathcliff must have looked, and the one time she had asked her father about the scene, when he had showed the movie for her brother when he was home on his first furlough, he had said the young man was the tennis pro at the club, and had been teaching her mother tennis, and she was such a natural that soon they had played together in tournaments. In the film they had just won the all-club tournament.

Soon her brother appeared, fat and blond and toddling stolidly around the big, flower-bordered back yard. Peyton knew that her mother had made these films, because in every one of them Buddy was attached in some way to his smiling father. Frazier McKenzie had been an attractive young man, Peyton thought, a little dour, maybe, with his long Scot's nose and sharp chin, and the peat-dark hair falling over his grey eyes, but when he laughed—and in the films he was almost always laughing—his face lit up with something powerfully magnetic, and he had a loose-limbed grace that made him seem a teenager. He almost was: Frazier McKenzie had married Lila Lee Peyton when he was twenty-two and she just eighteen. He had been only twenty-four when Buddy was born.

There followed an hour of Christmases and birthdays, in which Buddy stopped being the heavy-bottomed cherub and became the heavy-jawed, frowning young nimrod squinting into the distance with his first shotgun broken across his arm. And finally there she was, in a Christmas morning portrait posed before a big tree, along with her father and her brother. There she was, in the middle of the Christmas tinsel: a round melon, a knot of darkness in her mother's stomach, the cancer that would soon end the movies for good.

In the morning she got up and cut her hair. She did it swiftly and ruthlessly before the bathroom mirror, not meeting her own eyes, grasping each long braid and sawing it clumsily with the kitchen shears. She stood for a long moment, staring at the peat-brown ropes that had bound her to childhood, now lying on the worn linoleum, and then she lifted her head to the mirror. An apparition looked back. Her hair hung in tattered hanks around her pale face, stopping a few inches below her ears. Medusa, she thought. That's who I look like. Medusa. Well, then, OK. If they try to get all over me I'll turn them to stone. She grinned savagely, ran warm tap water over her hands, slicked it onto her hair and fluffed it out of its limp helmet. It has some curl in it. In her mind she saw soft, tumbling waves drifting around her head. They would make her eyes larger, soften her face, make her thin mouth bloom. She knew, as she looked into the mirror, that she hoped to see her mother there.

Medusa still looked back. How could the loss of two pigtails have made this malevolent difference? Peyton took a deep breath, said aloud, 'I don't give a damn,' and walked into the kitchen.

Clothilde was washing the breakfast dishes, her dark hands slipping in and out of the sinkful of steaming suds. She turned to look at Peyton and dropped the Fiestaware creamer into the water.

'Peyton, what in the name of God you done?' she breathed.

'Obviously, Clothilde, I have cut my hair. Maybe you've heard of haircuts?' Peyton said with a cold aluminium brightness.

'I heard of haircuts,' Chloe said. 'That ain't no haircut. That look like you took a lawnmower to it. Your daddy gon' have a fit. What was you thinkin' of?'

'I was tired of it,' Peyton said airily. 'Pigtails are for babies.'

'Well, your daddy gon' grow you up real quick,' Clothilde said fiercely, and then her dark face softened. 'Why don't you go try to do something with it, maybe wet it and push it back behind your ears, and let me tell him. Get him used to the notion. You can get Miss Freddie at the beauty shop to even it up some tomorrow afternoon.'

'Where is Daddy?' Peyton said in the new bright voice.

'He out in his office. You know, Peyton, you got that pretty straw hat Miss Augusta bought you for Easter. Why don't you wear it to Sunday School this morning? Maybe with your blue dress.'

'I'm not going to Sunday School or church,' Peyton said. 'I'm tired of that, too. I'm going to read all day. Sunday is a day of rest.'

She stalked out of the kitchen, and went into her room and closed the door. She waited all day for her father to come to her room. She had never done anything so overtly grotesque before, and she had no idea what he would do. She was afraid of his anger, but she was more afraid of simple, cold contempt. By supper time she could stand it no longer, so she smoothed the ragged spikes as best she could and went into the living room, where her father sat with the Sunday paper. He had lit only one lamp, which stood beside his cracked leather easy chair, and in its pale glow she could see only his profile.

'Peyton,' he said, not turning his head. His voice was weary.

'I guess you want to see it,' she said.

He turned his head and looked at her. He was silent for a long while. Peyton felt tears like acid rising in her throat.

'We haven't taken you very seriously, have we?' Frazier McKenzie said at last. His voice was still weary, but there was nothing in it of shock or anger. Perhaps it might still be all right . . .

'Daddy, it was a mistake, I don't know why I did it . . .'

'I don't care about your hair, Peyton,' he said. 'We can get that fixed; Augusta is going to take you into Atlanta and get you all prettied up. It's that you were so unhappy, and needed attention so much, and we didn't notice it—*I* didn't notice it. I wish you had come and talked to me about whatever is bothering you instead of chopping off your pretty hair, but I'm not exactly the kind of father a young girl comes running to, am I?'

The tears began to spill over Peyton's lower lashes. 'I'm not unhappy,' she quavered. 'I don't need attention. You're a good father, Daddy. I don't know why I did it. It just seemed all of a sudden something I needed to do . . . But it looks pretty awful, doesn't it?'

He gave a tired smile. 'You're a pretty girl, Peyton. I think you'll be a pretty woman one day. But we're going to have to make some changes. Augusta was right. You're at the point now where you need a woman in your life. You'll be thirteen in—June, isn't it? You can't be a child any more. You can't just run wild.'

'I don't run wild,' Peyton whispered, the unfairness of it loosening the tears again. 'I've never run wild in my life.'

'No, you haven't,' he said. 'It was a bad choice of words. But you've got to grow up some, and you've got to do it the right way. It's got to start now, and I can't do it, so on Tuesday your Aunt Augusta is taking you to Rich's for a hairdo and some clothes and maybe to lunch at the tearoom. You may find that you have a good time.'

'I won't,' Peyton cried, panic rising in her chest.

'You will,' he said, and he turned back to his newspaper.

Peyton went back to her room and threw herself across her narrow bed and cried in the winter twilight, knowing that change was upon her and it was going to be terrible, and that she and she alone had summoned it with a pair of kitchen shears.

2

Peyton went to school the next day with a scarf that had been her mother's tied under her chin. It was cream silk, splashed with huge red poppies and green vines, and must have looked festive and exotic on her mother. On Peyton, it looked almost shocking. But it was better than the hair. Peyton had it all planned: she would tell people she had an earache and had to keep the cold air off of it. 'We're going into Atlanta tomorrow to see a specialist,' she would say.

But no one asked and no one even mentioned the scarf.

After school she went straight to the Losers Club. When she came into the toolshed Ernie and Boot were waiting for her.

Peyton jerked the scarf off, heart surging up into her throat, and assumed the Betty Grable bathing-beauty pose. *'Taadaa!'* she cried.

'Holy cow!' Boot said reverently. 'You done won the stupidest prize for the next two years. You looks like a picked pullet, Peyton. What you go and do that for?'

'So I could win the stupidest prize for the next two years.'

'Well, it ain't no contest,' Boot said. 'What you daddy say?'

'He said it was very becoming.'

'Then he crazy as batshit,' Boot said mournfully.

Peyton looked at Ernie, who was sitting still and looking back at her. She knew he could flay her alive if he wished.

Ernie cocked his fuzzy head and studied her. 'You know, it's really not bad at all,' he said finally. 'You need to get it evened up a little, but I think you might look quite chic. Better than just pretty, really. Perhaps you're going to amount to something as a woman after all.'

Peyton felt a hopeful disbelief. Could he mean what he said? Of course not; anyone could see how she looked. But Ernie had never spared anyone's feelings before. She smiled, a silly, quivering smile.

Boot simply stared.

'Well, you little people run on now,' Ernie said. 'I've got to take Mama to the dentist. Maybe this time he'll drill her tongue out.'

Peyton laughed. The Losers Club had found its proper place in her firmament and her life was suddenly all right again.

It was early. No one would expect her home for a couple of hours yet, so she decided to go and see her grandmother. The walk took only about ten minutes. Her grandmother would understand, even if she didn't like the hair.

Peyton found Agnes McKenzie in her dim, cluttered kitchen, icing tea cakes. Nana always made them for Peyton, and they were sublime. A sweet vanilla smell told Peyton that there was another sheet of them in the old black woodstove. She stood still and breathed deeply. This was the very smell of childhood, rich and succouring.

Her grandmother did not turn round.

'Knew it was you,' she said. 'Saw it in the washtub this morning. Saw that you could do with a mess of tea cakes, too. Right now I need you to bring me some more wood in from the pantry.'

Peyton went into the pantry shed that opened off the kitchen. The wood basket stood there, along with a pristine electric stove and a new washer and dryer that Frazier had given to his mother two years before. Agnes McKenzie had never used them. She had simply thanked her son sweetly and gone on with heavy iron stove lids and dark soapy water. Only Peyton knew why.

'I see things in the fire and the water,' Agnes had told her once. 'The bad things in the fire and the good ones in the water. It's how I know things.'

Peyton picked up an armful of kindling and went back into the warm, dim kitchen.

'If you saw me in the water, that's good, isn't it?' Peyton said to her grandmother.

Agnes turned and looked at her, and then smiled. In the dimness she looked perhaps thirty, a smoky-haired, ocean-eyed thirty. Beautiful. Wild.

'Child,' she said. 'Look at you. I knew you'd lost something. I saw that in the fire. Come sit and we'll have coffee and tea cakes. There's not much that good strong coffee and tea cakes won't put right.'

Peyton took the cup gratefully and sipped the steaming coffee. She didn't like it very much—it was sludgy and bitter—but no one else let her have coffee. It made another bond with her grandmother.

'You look like you been whupped through hell with a buzzard gut, as our old washerwoman used to say,' Agnes said. 'But that doesn't matter. It won't last. You're going to be a handsome woman. You're going to look a lot like me, I think, when you get really old. And that's pretty good, if I do say so myself. What bothers me is why you did it.'

'I don't know,' Peyton said miserably, realising that she had been counting on her grandmother to say that she looked fine.

'Big change coming. Is that it?' Agnes said.

'I guess,' Peyton said. 'Everybody's going on about it. "You have to change, Peyton." "You won't have any boyfriends, Peyton."'

'You think making yourself ugly is going to change that? You'll grow up, my heart, ugly or not. Whacking off your hair isn't going to stop it.'

'Well, it just might put it off a while,' Peyton said, stung.

'Don't think so,' Agnes said. 'I see that it's right on top of you.'

'Do you see what's going to make me change? Daddy and Aunt Augusta are making me go to Rich's tomorrow and get styled and buy some new clothes. I think that's just the beginning . . .'

'I see a woman in your life, Peyton, for a long time to come. Yes. That much is clear.'

'Is it Aunt Augusta? Is it you?'

'I don't think it's Augusta. I wouldn't allow that, in any case. And it isn't me. I don't know who it is, only that she's coming.'

'Did you see her in the water or the fire?'

'I saw her in a bowl of Campbell's tomato soup.' Her grandmother smiled and reached out to touch the murdered hair gently. 'I don't know what that means. It doesn't feel like it's bad, though. Only . . . very different.'

WHEN PEYTON GOT HOME, she found the kitchen dark and the table still not set for supper. The house was very quiet. She listened hard, in faint unease. Then she heard the burring grumble of the old Electrolux upstairs somewhere, and followed the sound up.

She found Chloe vacuuming in the big upstairs back bedroom that they had always called the guest room, only Peyton could not remember any guests ever being in it. It would have been her room if she had not clung to her small one downstairs.

A thought rooted her in the doorway. They were making her move upstairs. It was a part of Aunt Augusta's adulthood campaign. Peyton darted into the room.

'What are you doing, Chloe?' she shouted. 'Because if anybody thinks they can make me move up here, they've got another think coming.'

Clothilde turned off the Electrolux. 'It ain't for you,' she said. 'We're going to have a guest in this room pretty soon.'

'A guest?' Peyton said stupidly. 'What guest?'

'Your Cousin Nora coming to see us. Your daddy called from

his office this afternoon. He said to get the room ready and to tell you he had to go into Atlanta to the courthouse this evening and not to wait up for him. Oh, and your Aunt Augusta said she'd pick you up at nine Wednesday morning, and to wear your Easter dress and straw hat.'

Peyton's head spun. 'What cousin? I never heard of any Cousin Nora. Who is she?'

'She your mama's younger cousin's girl,' Clothilde said. 'I never met her. Her mama and your mama had some kind of falling-out right after Miss Lila Lee and your daddy got married, and your mama didn't talk about her. I reckon Nora is your second cousin, and she'd be about thirty now. Seem to me they lived in Florida. I know she's coming in from Key West.'

Peyton felt a great gust of terror. 'How long is she going to stay?' she asked.

'Not long, I don't think. Your daddy say she on her way up north for a job. She just need a place to stop on the way.'

'There are about a million motels up on the interstate,' Peyton muttered. 'I don't want any visitors.'

Clothilde rolled her eyes. 'Why should she stay in a motel when she got folks here? Git on now, Peyton, and let me finish. I ain't even started supper yet.'

Peyton started to slam out of the room and then stopped. 'Chloe—Nana knew she was coming! She told me this afternoon there was a woman coming! She saw it in . . . the water.'

Peyton was not about to reveal that her grandmother had seen this troublesome cousin in a bowl of tomato soup.

'Huh. Most likely she saw it in a telephone,' Clothilde grumbled. 'You know your daddy call her every afternoon.'

'So when is she getting here?'

'I don't know. Two or three days, your daddy says. By the time she gets here you'll be all prettied up and have some new clothes and all. She'll look at her cousin and say, "Woo-woo!"'

It was Clothilde's most favoured superlative. Peyton hated it. She turned and stumbled down the stairs to her room. The important thing, she decided, was to manage never to meet her cousin.

'You have a little bitty head in proportion to your neck,' Mr Antoine said, squinting at Peyton in the mirror. 'And you're really long and thin through the waist and legs. I think we'll balance that with a cloud of curls. Really feminine and soft around your face—it's sort of sharp, isn't it? And maybe just a few highlights to bring out your nice eyes. How does that sound?'

Peyton, feeling pinheaded and as attenuated as an El Greco, did not answer. Indeed, since Aunt Augusta had picked her up that morning in her Lincoln, Peyton had said as little as was humanly possible without incurring her aunt's wrath.

Aunt Augusta was hovering behind the chair in Rich's Beauty Salon, where Peyton sat swathed in a pink drape, while Mr Antoine danced around her like a dervish, darting in to snip, fluff, stand back, snip again.

'So did you get bubble gum in your hair, or what?' he asked her as he snipped. 'I see that a lot. Not to worry. You left us plenty to work with. You're going to leave here looking like Sandra Dee.'

Peyton closed her eyes then. She did not open them as he worked in the permanent solution or when he pulled her hair onto rollers, or put her under the dryer. It seemed hours later when Mr Antoine shook her awake for what he called the comb-out. Peyton opened her eyes then, but she did not look into the mirror.

He combed and brushed and fluffed and sprayed, humming tunelessly as he worked. Finally Peyton heard him step back.

'*Voilà!*' he cried gaily. 'The new you. And just *look* at you!'

'Oh, Peyton, it looks just lovely,' Aunt Augusta trilled.

Peyton lifted her eyes, and her stomach lurched. All you saw was the hair. It was a tall, round helmet with a perfectly smooth exterior, inside which a surf of tiny curls and waves swirled.

And it was blonde. Butter yellow. Cadmium yellow.

'You're an entirely different person, Peyton,' her aunt said. 'There's absolutely nothing babyish about you now.'

Peyton could not speak. Were they both insane? Could neither of them see what they had done to her?

'Told you you'd love it,' Mr Antoine said, and he whirled away into another cubicle to answer a telephone.

'Truly, isn't it remarkable?' her aunt said happily, guiding Peyton out of the chair and towards the salon door.

'Yes,' Peyton whispered.

'I think we'll do a little something extra before lunch,' Augusta McKenzie said. 'Your hair is lovely, but it sort of overpowers your thin little face. I think we'll go down to Max Factor and get you made up. Nothing garish, of course, just a little blush and shadow and pink lipstick, to pop out those eyes and that mouth.'

Peyton found to her horror that she could do nothing but follow her aunt blindly out of the salon. Her legs trembled so that she could hardly stand, and she reached out and took her aunt's arm.

Augusta squeezed her hand. 'Well, this turned out to be fun, now, didn't it?' she said, smiling. 'You seem older already. We're like a couple of girls, skipping school and out for a shopping spree. I haven't had such fun in a long time.'

Peyton let her aunt lead her to the Max Factor counter as docilely as a lamb to the slaughterer's knife. There was nothing more they could do to her. Whatever they did would pale beside the hair. She sat down on a tall stool and closed her eyes again. She would endure. It would be over. They would go home. She would do something to the hair, something, anything.

Peyton felt a soft brush dancing over her face, and a thick smear of something that smelt like bubble gum being slicked onto her mouth. She went far away behind her closed eyes and waited.

At last her aunt caroled, 'Well, just look at our debutante!'

Peyton looked, blurring her eyes. She saw nothing but colour: the yellow aureole that she supposed was the hair, two pink blotches that must be blush, a slash of deeper pink that was undoubtedly lipstick.

'Wow,' she said, not really seeing.

'Wow, indeed,' her aunt said. 'Let's get you these things, and I can help you practise putting them on until you've got it down. It takes a little practice or it looks unnatural.'

'No kidding,' Peyton whispered. Another dreadful thing that could be fixed when she got home.

They ate frozen fruit salad and little chicken-salad sandwiches in the tearoom, then they stopped at the Tween Shop, a terrible place of posturing prepubescent mannequins with impossibly slim waists and gently swollen breasts, most wearing pencil strokes of pink or blue or yellow, a few in shirtwaisters with drifts of skirt and neat little collars and belts. A curly, flowered placard said that these offerings were suitable for young misses aged eleven to fourteen. Peyton knew that no matter what they put on her face or body, she wasn't ever going to look like the women of Rich's Department Store.

Aunt Augusta, accompanied by a clucking saleslady, dug among the racks of clothes like a terrier. She pulled out a horrifying cerise dress and jacket and a dark, plain sheath with a little coat to match. She selected two slim skirts and white blouses with little round collars, and a shirtwaister with tiny blue flowers and a little round collar.

'A Villager,' the saleslady said solemnly, as if she were offering a Fabergé egg. 'All the girls are buying them.'

Obediently, Peyton let Aunt Augusta and the saleslady lead her into a small cubicle walled with mirrors. She closed her eyes and let the legendary Villager slide over her rigid hair and down her body. She stood, desperately unfocused, as the saleslady buttoned up the front of the bodice and pulled the belt snug around her waist.

'If I might make a suggestion,' the saleslady said. 'There are some sweet preteen bras in Lingerie, with just a little light padding to give clothes some shape. Shall I just run over and pick a few out?'

'No,' Peyton all but wept. 'I won't wear one. I don't have anything to put in it. I wouldn't wear one if I did.'

Aunt Augusta raised her eyebrows at the saleslady and shook her head, smiling ruefully. The saleslady smirked back.

'Why don't you just pick out a couple that you think would be suitable and add them to my charge account?' Aunt Augusta said. 'I guess the smallest size they have. Do they make them small enough?'

'Oh yes. The sizes start at twenty-eight triple-A. Now, could I show you a little garter belt and some stockings?'

'I think I'm going to throw up,' Peyton said.

The trot to the rest room seemed endless. Swallowing hard against bile, Peyton plodded dumbly behind her aunt, who was leading her by the hand and saying, 'You can hold it, now. You know you don't want to throw up in the middle of Rich's . . .'

Peyton did hold it, but only just. She lurched into one of the stalls and vomited before she could even latch the door. When she finally stopped, she was weak and sweaty. She leaned against the cold steel of the cubicle and breathed in deep, desperate gasps.

Presently her aunt opened the cubicle and produced a handful of wet paper towels. She began to dab and scrub at Peyton's dress.

'Come on out here and let's wash your face,' she said. 'Oh, goodness. Just look at you. Your make-up is all smeared . . .'

Peyton stood mute, splashing her face in the sink when her aunt told her to, rinsing her mouth, letting Augusta pat her dry.

'Better now?' Augusta said. 'Your colour's coming back. Here, let's just touch you up a little. I wonder if it was that chicken salad—you're really not used to rich food. Come on, let's get you home. We'll get a Coca-Cola in the parking lot. That'll settle your tummy.'

Peyton followed Augusta out of the ladies' room and down the escalator to the basement parking lot. She sat there dumbly while their car was brought round, sipping the Coca-Cola her aunt bought her and knowing in her heart that there had been nothing asked of her, no test put to her, that she had not, on this day, failed.

IN THE LINCOLN Peyton put her head back against the seat and slept, waking only when the car stopped at last.

She opened her eyes slowly. Perhaps, if it was still early enough, she could get to her room and lock the door and begin the undoing of the horror before anyone saw her.

What she saw was her father and Clothilde, wrestling a mattress down the front steps and onto the lawn. Her father had on his white office shirt, but the sleeves were rolled and the collar was unbuttoned, and his hair fell over his face. Behind him, at the other end of the bouncing mattress, Chloe shone with sweat, like basalt.

Aunt Augusta tooted the horn gaily. 'Frazier McKenzie, come here and look at your grown-up daughter,' she trilled, and then she got out of the car the better to see the first viewing of her handiwork.

Peyton did not move. Her father shielded his face against the sun with his hand and walked slowly towards her side of the car. When he reached it he stopped and stared in. Peyton met his eyes and saw in them sheer shock and revulsion. They were gone in an instant, replaced by a smile, but they had been there.

'Well, my goodness,' he said. 'Get out and let's have a look at you.'

Peyton sat rooted in the Lincoln.

'She's had a little upset tummy,' Aunt Augusta offered across the roof of the Lincoln. 'She probably needs some iced tea and a nap. But first we're going to have a fashion show . . .'

Peyton jerked her door open and leapt out and ran past her father and the wide-eyed Clothilde and into the house, and into her room, and closed her door. She heard the murmur of voices out on the lawn, a hum like bees, with an occasional fragment of a sentence spiking up: '. . . at least she might have said thank you. Look, she's just left all these new things in the car. Frazier, I really think . . .'

Then her father's voice: '. . . maybe a little extreme for her age, Augusta. Let her get used to it. Let *us* get used to it. Good Lord, I didn't even recognise her.'

'Well, I guess ingratitude runs in the family,' she heard her aunt huff, and after that the solid thunk of the Lincoln's door closing.

She crawled onto her bed and pulled the faded afghan that her grandmother had made for her at her birth up over her ears. She did not move for a long, long time. By the time Chloe came to her door, her windows had darkened with the still-winter twilight.

'Peyton, you come on out to supper now,' Chloe called. 'Your daddy gone to a meeting up to the church, he say he want to see you before you go to bed. He say he think you looks pretty as a princess, and he wants to tell you himself. And I think we can fix that hair so it ain't so hard, and take some of that stuff off your face. It's gon' be all right. Come on out now, and after supper you can show me your new clothes. Your aunt left them for you.'

Peyton did not reply. Presently Clothilde went heavily away.

She was back in an hour. 'I got to go home,' she said. 'Ain't nobody with Boot. I'm settin' this tray right outside your door.

You stop actin' like a baby now and come on out and eat it. Your Cousin Nora comin' tomorrow. You don't want her to think you a baby in a tantrum.'

Peyton still did not reply. She heard Clothilde mutter, and soon the closing of the front door, and then silence and darkness fell over the house. Peyton padded to her door and opened it and pulled the tray inside so that her father would not see it sitting there, set it on her desk and crawled back into her bed.

She heard her father at her door some time later, dimly. 'Peyton, you awake?' he called softly.

She did not answer. She lay motionless until at last, aeons later, she heard him click off the television and start up the stairs to bed. She waited another hour, and then she got up and tiptoed through the dark to the downstairs bathroom and ran a tub of water. She ran it very slowly so that her father would not hear it thundering into the porcelain tub.

When the bath was full Peyton got in and submerged herself. She felt the hair helmet soften stickily. She got the Ivory soap from the soap dish and scrubbed her head until it stung. The water around her yellowed. Some kind of rinse, then. Good.

She scrubbed herself all over, then got out of the tub, wrapped her hair in a towel, dressed in jeans and a T-shirt, and stole back to her room. She sat down in front of the maple dressing table and closed her eyes for a long time, and then she jerked the towel away. A towering mound of dun-coloured Brillo sat atop her head, lightless and dense. She could not get her comb through it.

Peyton got up, took the afghan and a pillow from her bed, and went out of her room. She got an apple, some cheese and a Coca-Cola from the refrigerator and went outside and climbed the dogwood tree where her father had constructed a shelter for her, more elaborate than a platform but less so than a roofed tree house. It had railings and one solid wall against the tree trunk. Two years before she had dragged an old air mattress up there, and now she propped her pillow on it, and lay down and covered herself with her afghan.

She prepared to cry, but instead she slept.

SHE AWOKE WITH A JOLT. Pearly morning light was streaming through the tree's bare branches, and her father was calling her from the ground.

'Come down from there right now, Peyton.' His voice was both cold and weary.

Clothilde's voice joined his, shrill and angry. 'Well, I hope you happy,' she squalled. 'Your cousin here waitin' to meet you, and you stuck up in that tree like an ol' possum. She drove all night, she say. You git down from there this minute.'

Peyton did not look down at them, and she did not answer. She unfocused her eyes and squinted instead out towards the street. A blur of pure, shocking flamingo pink flamed there against the asphalt. She brought it into focus. It was a Thunderbird coupé, a fairly old one, from what she knew of those exotic cars, covered with road dust, but still fabulous in the morning light. Nobody in Lytton had a Thunderbird.

There was a creak of the steps to the tree house, and a woman's face appeared over its edge. It was freckled with copper and long and sharp-chinned, and a thick sheaf of dark red hair fell over one of its pale green eyes. It was an exaggerated face, almost a grotesque one, and Peyton simply stared. Then the mouth quirked up into a smile, and it was transformed into something near beauty.

'Dr Livingstone, I presume?' the woman said, and her voice was as slow and rich as cooling fudge, with a little hill of laughter in it. It was a wonderful voice, magical.

The woman swung herself up onto the platform and sat down, legs crossed, chin on hands. Her arms and legs were long, and in her blue jeans she was very thin. She looked solemnly at Peyton. Peyton stared back, as mesmerised as a cobra in a fakir's basket.

'I'm your Cousin Nora Findlay. I've driven all night to meet you, and I'm tired and I need my breakfast, and I want you to have yours with me. I don't have any other cousins. Then we'll do something about that hair. Sweet Jesus, what on earth were they thinking?'

Peyton put her head down and began to cry, and her Cousin Nora pulled her over and held her until Peyton had cried herself out, and then they climbed down the tree to breakfast.

3

The first thing you noticed about Nora Findlay, Peyton thought, was that she gave off heat, a kind of sheen, like a wild animal. There was a padding, hip-shot prowl to her walk, and she moved her body as if she were totally unconscious of it. She had a long Roman nose and a full mouth and with her slanted yellow-green eyes and thick, tumbled red hair, Peyton thought she looked like some sort of wildcat: a leopard, a ruddy puma, a cheetah.

Clothilde had bacon and eggs waiting for them in the yellow breakfast room. Peyton had a couple of hours yet before school. She would have liked to retreat to her room and think about the enormities of the past twelve hours, especially this strange, leonine cousin who had arrived in a pink chariot and laid siege to her tree. But she did not dare. Disapproval shone out of Chloe's face like steam off asphalt, and she could still hear the steel in her father's voice. She was in disgrace. There was nothing for it but to sit down at the blue lacquered table and wait for what would come. For a long time no one spoke, and she did not raise her eyes from her plate. There was only the chink of silver on china as Nora ate.

She smelt cigarette smoke then, an alien smell in this house, and she looked up at her cousin. Nora was smoking a cigarette from the fresh pack of Salems that sat on the table beside her.

'Have I broken a taboo?' she said in the rich, slow voice. 'Am I going to have to sneak behind the woodshed to smoke?'

She swept the heavy hair off her face with one long hand and turned to Peyton. 'Might as well join you in Coventry,' she said. 'Two's company, they say.'

'Coventry?' Peyton said in a small, tight voice.

'It means disgrace. For some reason, being sent to Coventry means the ultimate punishment; it means shunning. I don't know why. It means we're both of us in deep shit.'

Peyton gasped. She had never heard such a word used in this

house. It hung in the warm air, and in the ensuing silence she heard a snorted 'Huh!' from Clothilde that meant her direst disapproval. She wondered if Chloe would tackle Nora directly.

'I'm sorry, Clothilde,' Nora called out. 'I hope I haven't blotted my copybook too badly.' She smiled into the kitchen at Chloe.

'It ain't like I never heard "shit" before,' Chloe said. 'It just that Mr Frazier ain't gon' want Peyton to hear it.'

'It's not like I haven't heard it before, either,' Peyton surprised herself by saying. And then she looked down at her plate and blushed. She would speak no more to this usurping stranger. Her cousin was not going to charm her with sweet cigarette smoke and soft 'shits'.

Nora finished her coffee. She stretched and yawned and said, 'I have never eaten a better breakfast. I mean that, Clothilde. It is all right if I call you that?'

'What else you gon' call me?' Chloe grumbled, but there was a smile at the corners of her black eyes.

'I'm bushed,' Nora said, getting up from the chair. Peyton saw that she wore tennis shoes over bare feet, and that her feet were small and neat, out of all proportion to her height.

'You upstairs in the back bedroom on the right,' Clothilde said. 'Mr Frazier said to let you sleep as long as you wanted to, that he'll see you for dinner. See all of us, I means.'

Peyton would not look up. She felt rather than saw her cousin come round to stand behind her chair. In a moment Nora's long hands were cupping her head, smoothing back the electric hair, pulling it sleekly behind her head and winding it.

'Got bobby pins, Chloe?' Nora said, and Chloe produced some from somewhere in her vast necessities drawer. There was a final tug and the feeling of the bobby pins slipping firmly home, and then Nora took Peyton's shoulders and stood her up and led her to the old mirror over the oak chest that held linens and silver.

'What do you think?'

Peyton looked. A small face under a smooth crown of hair looked back at her, sitting atop a long neck that seemed, now, slender instead of scrawny, and round the sharp chin and slanted cheekbones a few wisps of the horrendous curls lay softly. The image was not appalling. But it was not her. She merely stared.

'It's a French twist,' Nora said. 'It's not really right for you, but it gets that mess off your face and shows off those fabulous bones. If you like, we'll work on it some more tonight.'

Still Peyton stared.

Nora gave her shoulders a small shake, then went up the dim staircase towards her room.

Only then did Peyton look at Clothilde.

'That's right nice, Peyton,' Chloe said. 'Shows off them eyes.'

'I hate it,' Peyton said, but there was no heat in her voice. She went into her little room to get dressed for school, and for the first time in her life she felt almost confident, almost anticipatory, about going into the swarm of flips and bouffants that awaited her.

Nobody's got a French twist, she thought. This ought to shut up a few of them. Of course, I'm not going to keep it . . .

She realised as she walked to school that she could not wait to show her new hair to the Losers Club that afternoon.

But it was not her hair that the Losers Club wanted to talk about. They did not even mention it. Instead the subject was, first, her night in the tree, and, second, her Cousin Nora Findlay.

'Guess you gets the stupid prize, Peyton,' Boot said, eating Planter's peanuts out of the big can from which Ernie doled a grudging inch or two for each of them once or twice a week.

For the first time, Peyton felt no hummingbird dart of triumph in her chest. She felt cross, waspish. The night before had been a source of stunning pain and revelation to her. She was not going to have it cut down to the status of stupidity of the week.

'It wasn't stupid. It was something I planned, a protest. I'm proud of it,' she said.

'I should think you might make your point better face to face,' Ernie drawled, but Peyton knew somehow that he envied her her flight into the dogwood tree. She realised then that Ernie would never dare leave his mother to go and sit in a tree all night.

'OK, so it ain't stupid. Tell about your cousin,' Boot said. 'I heard she redheaded as a woodpecker and ain't got no brassiere.'

'She has long red hair like a waterfall and green eyes, and real long legs, and she smokes Salems. As for the brassiere, I don't know about that.'

In Peyton's mind, her Cousin Nora was rapidly being transmuted into something fabulous, a unicorn, a young griffin.

'How did y'all know about that stuff last night?' she said.

'Huh. Half of Lytton probably know it by now,' Boot said.

When Peyton got home, Nora was nowhere in sight, but her Aunt Augusta was, sitting at the breakfast table with a cup of coffee and a slice of Clothilde's pineapple upside-down cake. She was stabbing the cake and waving it on her fork and haranguing Chloe at the same time.

Chloe ironed on, unconcerned and uncommunicative. Every now and then she would say, 'Uh-*uh*,' when Augusta made a point, or 'I don't know nothin' about that, Miss Augusta.'

Peyton tried to slip past her back and into her own room, but Aunt Augusta rounded on her.

'Well, so here's our grown-up little lady,' she said with heavy sarcasm. 'The one who, by now, the whole town knows spent the night in a tree after her daddy and her aunt bent over backward to fix her up some. If your daddy doesn't listen to me now about boarding school, I'll be mighty surprised. Just look at that hair! Now what did you do to it?'

'It's a French twist,' Peyton said coldly. 'My cousin fixed it for me. She's going to fix it some more when she wakes up.'

Peyton had completely forgotten that she herself had planned to murder the French twist as soon as she could get to a mirror. In a heartbeat it became a powerful amulet against Aunt Augusta.

'Everybody at school loved it,' she lied. 'Grace Kelly wore one at her wedding. Some of the girls said I looked just like her.'

None of this was true, but Peyton did not care.

For a moment her aunt was speechless. Then she recovered.

'Oh, yes, your Cousin Nora,' she said venomously. 'Who drove in here at daybreak in a dirty pink convertible, with her shorts rolled up to her whatever, and got in bed and slept all day. Oh, yes, that's just wonderful. What a shining example. When I think what her mother did to your mother, when I think what little tramps those Vandiver women were, I shouldn't be surprised at anything this one does.'

'What do you mean, what her mother did to my mother?' Peyton said in a small voice.

'Well, it's time you knew,' her aunt huffed. 'Her mother stole your mother's fiancé away from her and ran off with him, and we all heard that she had your famous Cousin Nora way before she ever married that no-good Creighton Findlay. Not that that little affair lasted long; he walked out on her before Nora was two years old. After that she lived all over the place, with one relative or another, dragging that child with her. I guess it's no wonder . . . anyway, she and the child lived with almost every Peyton and Vandiver family except your mama and daddy. Your mama never spoke to her after that business with Creighton Findlay.'

'My mother's fiancé?' Peyton said. 'You mean . . . not Daddy?'

'Of course not! Your daddy is worth a million Findlays. He met and married your mother just after that. It was the saving of her. Creighton Findlay was as no-good as they come, but he was a handsome devil and she was crazy about him.'

'My mother's cousin—Nora's mother—where is she?'

'She died in a sanatorium for alcoholics in St Petersburg, Florida,' Aunt Augusta said with satisfaction.

'Not so,' a black-coffee voice said from the stairs. 'Everybody knows she married the Emperor of Bhutan and is living in splendour in the shadow of Everest. I see her often.'

Nora padded into the breakfast room, smiling amiably at Aunt Augusta, her green eyes slitted and her mane of hair tangled. She wore a long T-shirt that said 'Jesus Is Coming. Look Busy', and obviously nothing else. She smiled at Aunt Augusta.

'Well, Nora,' her aunt said, extravagantly avoiding looking at the Jesus T-shirt and the bobbling wealth of Nora underneath it.

'Well, Cousin Augusta,' Nora said, the smile widening as she sat down opposite Aunt Augusta at the breakfast table.

'How long do you plan to be with us?' Augusta McKenzie said.

Peyton could not imagine that anyone could miss the animosity in her aunt's voice, but Nora seemed to. She smiled sleepily. 'I hadn't thought, really,' she said. 'I just got here. I'd like to look around Lytton some. And then I'd like to see Atlanta.'

'Frazier said you were on your way to a job?' Aunt Augusta said. 'What sort of job might that be?'

'Clothilde, do you think I might possibly have a sliver of that cake?' Nora said, smiling into the kitchen. 'It smells like pure heaven. Well, I don't have any specific plans, Cousin Augusta. I'm just looking around to see what's what.'

Chloe brought the cake and poured a cup of strong, hot coffee for Nora. 'More where that came from,' she said.

Nora smiled her thanks around a mouthful of cake and rolled her eyes. 'Bliss,' she said. 'Nirvana. Maybe you could teach me to cook while I'm here. I really don't have any domestic skills.'

'What *are* your skills, Nora?' Aunt Augusta said. 'We never exactly knew.'

'Well, I'm good at English, and I write a little. I've been teaching for the past few years, in Miami and Key West. I've enjoyed that. I taught special English classes to Cuban and Haitian children.'

'Oh, really?' Augusta's nostrils flared as if she had smelt something dreadful. 'Coloured children, you mean?'

'Oh, yes. Black as the ace of spades, some of them. It was a real revelation for me to get acquainted with such different cultures.'

'Well, you won't find much opportunity for that kind of thing here,' Augusta said.

'Oh, really?' Nora said. 'I've already seen quite a few black people around here. Surely their children go to school?'

'Not our school,' Aunt Augusta said. 'They have their own school, and it's a good one. Frazier is on their school board, just as he is on ours.'

'Strange,' muttered Nora, looking ingenuously up at Aunt Augusta. 'I thought *Brown versus Board of Education* must be fairly familiar around the South. Hasn't the news gotten to Lytton yet?'

'There's no need to be sarcastic,' Augusta snapped. 'That desegregation rule is all about choice. None of our coloured people have chosen to come to Lytton Grammar and High Schools. And why should they? Their own school is just fine.'

'Maybe I'll apply there, then.' Nora smiled. 'You asked about my skills, Cousin Augusta? I am a truly superior lay. Maybe the best lay east of the Rockies. Lots of people say so. Although it doesn't look like there's much market for that in Lytton. Oh, well. We shall see.'

Peyton stared, her mouth open, and Chloe snorted.

Aunt Augusta got up from her chair, wheeled on her sensible heel, and sailed in palpitating silence out of the room. Peyton heard the front door slam. She could not speak and only continued to stare.

Nora reached over and ruffled her hair. 'I'm really not all that good,' she said. 'At least I don't think I am. I don't consider it a skill, more a pleasure. But when I saw your aunt I thought, "Now there's a lady with very little to occupy her time, and I think maybe this will do it for a good while to come." Now'—and she looked at Clothilde—'how long do we have before Cousin Frazier gets home? I need to bathe and change.'

'He be home in about an hour,' Chloe said, and Peyton saw with astonishment that she was trying to hide a smile.

'Good,' Nora said, and she went back up the stairs.

Peyton turned to Chloe. 'You like her, don't you?' she said.

'Don't know her yet,' Chloe said. 'But she kind of like a fresh little breeze in here.'

Peyton slumped out of the kitchen to her room and threw herself on the bed to think about everything that had happened since the morning. Instead she slid so deeply into sleep that when her father came to wake her for supper she did not, for a moment, know where she was.

THEY ATE THAT EVENING in the big dining room off the other side of the kitchen, and Nora had dressed for the occasion. Her hair was up in a burnished French twist, and she wore a pink oxford-cloth shirt with the sleeves rolled up and a pink plaid madras skirt that wrapped around and tied. She looked, Peyton thought, like money, though she could not have said how. According to Aunt Augusta, Nora did not have a pot to piss in.

She liked her cousin best in shorts and T-shirt, she realised. This woman—for in the candlelight she looked like the woman she must be—had no connection with her.

Candlelight. The table set with heavy old silver, crystal glasses and the good china that had been her mother's. Peyton hated all of it. Her father had bidden it for this unknown cousin, when he had never bidden it for her, not even on her birthdays.

When Clothilde came in with plates of pot roast and mashed potatoes, her father said, 'This was a good idea, Chloe. I'd forgotten how nice this room is. We ought to do this more often.'

So it had been Chloe's idea, then. It made no difference to Peyton. She was not going to forgive her cousin. If it had not been for her, they would be eating pot roast comfortably in the breakfast room.

'I can't tell you what a perfect dinner this is,' Nora said. 'I've gotten so accustomed to getting my own meals that I'd forgotten what a pleasure good food and a beautiful table could be.'

'What do you usually eat?' Peyton said, forgetting to sulk.

'Pizza,' Nora said, smiling at her. 'Hamburgers. Kentucky Fried Chicken. Anything I can take with me in the car.'

'Oh,' Peyton said. 'Why don't you just stay home and eat?'

'Well, I'm not really sure where that is right now.'

'You must have a home. Everybody lives somewhere,' Peyton pushed it. Her father's eyebrows rose.

'I've lived a lot of places,' her cousin said, her face serene. She was, Peyton knew, going to refuse to be baited. 'I've lived all over Florida, and in Cuba for a while, and California. I realised I was getting sort of old for that kind of thing, and I thought I ought to look and see if I could find a nest somewhere. I'd like to settle for a while.'

'Nora taught coloured children,' Peyton said, looking sidewise to see how her father would take it. In the Deep South of her time, change had not even swept a wing over the small towns, and the federal government be damned.

'A good thing to do,' Frazier McKenzie said. 'There are never enough qualified teachers for the children who need them most.

I've often wondered what's going to happen to us if we don't educate all our children.'

Peyton goggled, her mouth full of apple cobbler. She had no idea that her father thought about things like that.

'I thought I might find some kind of minority teaching job around Atlanta,' Nora said. 'What with Dr King and all, it's the real epicentre of the Movement. It's what I do best, what I love.'

Her father looked at her cousin thoughtfully. 'When was it that your mother died?' he said.

'A long time ago,' she said. 'About twelve years. I hadn't lived with her for a while. You know she was sick? She drank an awful lot, and it got so that she couldn't take care of me or herself. One of my father's sisters put her in an institution, and I lived with her family for a year or two. Then I got a scholarship and went to Rollins, and I've essentially been on my own ever since. Don't worry about me, Cousin Frazier. I'm absolutely accustomed to taking care of myself. I'll find a place in Atlanta. I'm looking forward to it.'

'It would be nice to have you that close to us,' her father said. 'I know Lila Lee would want Peyton to know her cousin.'

'I'm sure,' Nora said, looking down.

When Chloe had taken away the last of the dishes, her father said to Nora, 'I usually watch a little TV after dinner. You're welcome to join me. Peyton's going to be doing her homework.'

'I'd love to,' Nora said.

'I don't have any homework,' Peyton said.

'I think you probably do,' her father said, and he rose from his chair. He held Nora's chair as she stood up. Peyton got up from hers and went through the kitchen and the breakfast room to her room. She was suddenly tired, but she did not sleep. Her father would be in, she knew. There was no escaping it. There would be an accounting for her actions of the night before.

She heard the television set go on, and then, a little later, incredibly, she heard her father laughing. Nora's rich laughter followed.

I hate her, Peyton thought clearly and roundly.

When her father came in at last, she was awake. He sat down on the edge of her bed. His face looked cold, carved from granite in the low lamplight.

'Peyton, last night was not acceptable,' he said. 'I've gone to bat for you with your aunt more times than you know, but after this I've got to admit she's right. You've got to have some supervision.'

'No,' Peyton whispered.

'Yes. Nothing like it can happen again, and I can't seem to prevent it. So here are your options. One, you can go to boarding school. Two, I can put you entirely in your Aunt Augusta's hands. You'd live here, of course, but she would decide what was best for you and see that you did it.'

Peyton felt tears of enormity and betrayal well into her eyes.

'Three,' her father said, 'your Cousin Nora can stay with us for a while and oversee things. I've asked her if she would consider it, and she's said she'll think about it.'

'Nora would mean more work for Chloe,' Peyton whispered miserably. 'And it'll cost you a lot extra.'

'She'll be finding a job around here. She's adamant about that.'

'You'll have to talk to her. You don't like to do that.'

'Nora's pleasant to talk to. Besides, I work most nights.'

Peyton was silent. It was no contest. Boarding school was unimaginable, Aunt Augusta too terrible to contemplate.

Her father got up and walked to her door and then stopped and looked back. 'Incidentally, I like your hair that way,' he said. 'I can see more than a little of your mother in you.'

Peyton turned off her bedside lamp. She burrowed under her covers, feeling warmth that came from somewhere inside her as well as out. For the first time in a long time, she did not show herself her movies.

PEYTON GOT UP EARLY the next morning and shuffled into the kitchen, patting her hair. She had not combed it since Nora fixed it for her and was halfway hoping her cousin would offer to refresh it. Peyton had no idea how to make a French twist.

'Where is everybody?' she said grumpily to Chloe, who emerged from the kitchen bearing a gluey mass of oatmeal. 'I *hate* that stuff, Chloe; you know I do. You wouldn't dare serve it if Daddy was here.'

'It ain't your daddy needs fattening up,' Chloe said, banging down the dish in front of Peyton. 'Your daddy's gone to a breakfast meeting of the school board up at the café, and Nora took off early this morning. Say she want to get a look at the town before it has a chance to get a look at her.'

'Did she take the Thunderbird?'

'She sho' did. You could hear that little old car peeling off a mile away. She got the top down and the radio going full blast, and she singing along with it. Town gon' get a look at her, all right.'

'They'll kick her out of here,' Peyton said with obscure satisfaction, not realising that she hoped this would not happen until after Nora fixed her hair.

'I 'spect Nora could kick back right good,' Chloe said. 'I'd hate to be the one who tries to run her off.'

'Do you know when she's coming back?' Peyton asked.

'She say she be back late this afternoon. We gon' eat a little early. She going into Atlanta to see a movie later on.'

'What movie? Is Daddy going with her? Am I going?'

'I think she mean to go by herself.'

'All the way up there at *night*?'

'Nora almost thirty years old,' Chloe said. 'And she done drive that car from one end of this country to the other. I 'spect she be OK at a movie in Atlanta.'

'Huh,' Peyton grumped, but in her mind she could see it: the little pink car slicing through the dark towards the smear of light that was the city, Nora with the red hair flaming out behind her. Something in her heart squeezed.

It was a strange day in school. At recess one of the senior boys, an Adonis so exalted by position on the football team as to be near sacred, said, 'Hey, Peyton, I hear your cousin came to see you and that she's a good-looking broad. You tell her that any time she wants a real man's company she can call me. I bet we'd get along real good.'

Peyton, who would have passed by this icon a day earlier with her eyes averted, looked him in the face. 'Don't hold your breath,' she said. 'She's got about a million boyfriends.'

'She really got a pink T-bird?' said one of the Adonis's appendages.

'Yeah, she does,' Peyton said grandly. 'We're taking it into Atlanta tonight to a movie. She's going to teach me to drive it.'

There was no reply, and she walked away, floating on power.

NORA DID NOT EAT dinner with them, but she sat at the table smoking and chatting pleasantly. She wore an astonishing outfit of tight black ankle-length pants and a loose, heavily embroidered blouse of some rough, gauzy material, and her hair was down again. It shone like molten copper in the light from the brass overhead lamp.

'I'll get something after the movie,' she said when Frazier McKenzie raised an eyebrow at her empty plate. 'I ate lunch real late, and I hear there's a nice little Italian restaurant next door to the movie theatre. I haven't had clam linguine for a long time.'

'Neither have I,' Frazier said. 'Maybe we'll all go sometime. I don't think Peyton has ever tasted clam linguine.'

'I've had clams,' Peyton said. 'I've had them at Howard Johnson's. I think they're overrated. I find that most seafood is.'

Even she could hardly believe the affected sentences coming out of her mouth. She looked up at Nora, expecting laughter.

Nora only smiled. 'That's because you've never had it fresh, right out of a tropical sea, and cooked over an outside grill, or made into a soup. I agree with you, frozen fried seafood is ghastly. I'll make you my special *sopa caliente* one day. That ought to change your mind about seafood.'

'What's in it?'

'Oh, rice. Sweet potatoes. Fresh coconut milk. Crab and langouste—little warm-water lobsters. Chunks of fish. Broth. Spices that I can't even pronounce. I brought some with me when I left Miami. I learned to make it when I lived in Cuba.'

'It sounds hideous,' Peyton said.

Her father gave her a look. 'It sounds good to me,' he said.

'Might make a nice change from southern cooking, not that Chloe doesn't do that better than anybody. Sometimes I think we just don't get out into the world enough down here in Lytton.'

Nora stubbed out her Salem in the ashtray Chloe had put at her place—two days and already it was her place, Peyton thought resentfully—and lit another. Then she put that out, too.

'This can be pretty offensive if nobody else in the house smokes,' she said. 'I'll confine it to my room, or go out on the porch.'

'No, don't bother,' Frazier said, and Peyton frankly goggled. 'I used to smoke. I still keep a pipe out in my office. I think smoke after a meal smells good. Maybe I'll bring it in and we can smoke Peyton out of here.'

Peyton stared. Her head spun. Her father, smoking? Cigarettes, a pipe? This cool, abstemious man?

'So, did you have a tour of Lytton like you planned?' her father asked. 'It must have taken you all of twenty minutes. What did you do with the rest of your day?'

'I spent the whole day around town,' she said. 'It's a charming little town, Frazier. I looked into both churches and walked into all the neighbourhoods. The houses aren't grand, but they're so neat, so right somehow. Roses on trellises, and vegetable gardens . . . It feels like nothing bad could ever happen here.'

You ought to try Lytton Grammar School, Peyton thought grimly.

'It's a pretty little town,' her father said mildly. 'But there are a lot of things that need changing here.'

'You mean like the "Coloured" and "White" entrances to the movie theatre? Maybe you could start with those.'

'It'll come,' he said. 'But it's going to have to come in its own time. If you tried to force that kind of change on Lytton all at once you'd hit a brick wall. Nothing would ever change.'

'But Frazier, it's the law of the land.'

Her father put down his coffee cup. 'Yes. It is,' he said. 'And we're lucky to have those laws in place at last. There's great change going on in the cities; you know that. But out here, in the backwaters, we're a hundred years behind the cities. It's going to be a matter of years. It's going to happen one mind at a time, one heart at a time. Meanwhile, we try, and we measure our victories in inches.'

Nora regarded him thoughtfully. 'Like what?'

'Well, like something I want to talk to you about. We talked about it at the school-board meeting this morning. The county education folks are about to get all over us for making no move towards compliance, and if they do that they'll never get any. So I thought—*we* thought—that a compromise might work for a while. Maybe one shared class, maybe an honours class so that everyone could see the idea working. You could hold it one week at Lytton High and the next at Carver High, and so on. I think maybe, once it got going, everybody might be able to live with that.'

'What kind of class?' Nora said.

'What do you think of English? An honours English class that maybe addressed the literature of blacks and whites alike. A small class, so there could be a lot of discussion . . .'

Nora raised her head. The bell of coppery hair swung forward over part of her face. 'I want that class, Frazier,' she said.

'I thought you might,' he said. 'I sold you and the class as a package. I said you might be willing to do some intensive tutoring, too. The black children are going to need it.'

'I would *love* it,' Nora breathed. 'It's just what I've hoped I'd find, but I never dreamed it could be here. When will you know?'

'The chairman's going to take it to the county meeting this next week, but I don't anticipate any problems. The county is going to be so relieved to see that we're making some sort of effort.'

'Of course I'd get my own place,' Nora said excitedly.

'No, we'd want you here if you'll stay,' her father said. 'That is, if you're still willing to spend some time with Peyton.'

'I can't think of anything I'd like more,' Nora said. 'We will teach each other wondrous things. As long as we all understand that I'm not trying to be a mother or a disciplinarian. Just a friend.'

'It's all we ask, isn't it, Peyton?' Her father was smiling.

'Uh-huh,' she said.

'So I'll let you know as soon as I do,' her father said. 'But I should think you might plan on starting in a couple of weeks.'

They sat in silence for a time, and then Nora said, 'I met your grandmother today, Peyton. Your mother,' and she nodded at Frazier, who grimaced.

'I can't wait to hear about that,' he said.

'Well,' Nora said. 'I was sitting on a bench in the square reading a book and this old lady sat down beside me. She looked at me and said, "I know you. I saw you coming in a bowl of tomato soup."'

'Oh, Lord,' Frazier said. 'I hope she didn't bother you.'

'God, no.' Nora giggled. Unlike the rich laugh, it was silvery, flutelike. Peyton felt the corners of her own mouth tug upwards. 'I thought she was fabulous. How many of us have been foreseen in a bowl of tomato soup? We talked about some amazing things. Then she raised her fist at a limb full of crows over by the railroad tracks and yelled, "Go tell the Devil!" and they flew off and so did she. I like her better than anybody I've met except you all.'

'That's a folk tale. She's Scottish,' Peyton said.

'I know the tale. I loved hearing somebody actually say it. I'll bet the Devil is getting an earful right now.'

Peyton looked at her keenly to see if she was making fun of her grandmother, but there was no indication of that. Nora's face was soft with enjoyment.

'How did you know she was my grandmother?' Peyton said.

'Oh, she introduced herself. But I'd have known anyway. You look just like her, Frazier, and you're probably going to, Peyton. I thought she was beautiful.'

'I'm glad you got along,' Frazier said almost primly.

'I'm going down to see her sometime over the weekend. She wants to ride in my car. Peyton, you come, too, if you want to.'

'I have a lot of homework,' Peyton said. Was this amoeba-like cousin going to absorb her grandmother, too?

Presently Nora got up and gathered up a huge straw bag and went out into the twilight, jingling her car keys. Peyton and her father sat in silence while the engine growled into life and then faded away down the street.

'Are you glad she's going to stay awhile?' her father asked her.

'I don't know,' Peyton mumbled.

4

In the night Peyton was woken by the crash of thunder and pelting rain. Before she fell back asleep she heard the slam of a car door and the pounding of footsteps on the front porch, then the softer opening and closing of the front door. Nora, coming back from Atlanta. It was, Peyton knew, very late. Her father wasn't going to like this one little bit.

Peyton, lulled by rain and the absence of sunlight filtering through her blinds, slept late and woke up cross and disorientated. She wrapped herself in her grandmother's afghan and stumbled into the breakfast room, trailing the afghan, blinking into the overhead lamplight.

'Tell Mr De Mille I'm ready for my close-up now,' Nora said from her seat at the table. She was smoking and smiling at Peyton. Her face, too, was crumpled with sleep, and her hair poured into her eyes like a sheepdog's. She wore a black silk kimono, belted tight and crawling with scarlet and gold dragons and tigers.

'Who's Mr De Mille?' said Peyton thickly, slumping down into her seat and looking at the cuckoo clock on the wall. It said ten fifteen. Outside, the aqueous light looked like dawn.

'It's from a movie called *Sunset Boulevard*,' Nora said, inhaling deeply and letting the smoke drift luxuriously from her nostrils. 'It's one of the great movies of all time. Gloria Swanson said that line. Next time it's at an art theatre, I'll take you.'

'Huh,' Peyton said, poking at the curling strips of bacon and the scrambled eggs on her plate. 'I was going to ride my bike down to Nana's today. But it looks like it's going to rain for the next hundred years.'

'I'll take you later,' Nora said. 'Right now we are going up to my room and I am going to fix that hair. Don't argue. It looks like a bird's nest caught in a windstorm.'

Peyton followed her cousin up the stairs to the big back bedroom without protesting, mainly because her hair did indeed look like a fright wig.

Nora sat her down in front of the mirror at the old walnut dressing table that had been there ever since Peyton could remember. Formerly it had worn only yellowing antimacassars and a vase of dried flowers. Now it was littered with bottles and tubes and brushes, and smelt of spilt powder and cologne. Despite herself, Peyton studied the array of cosmetics. There had been none in this house but her father's aftershave since her birth.

'I'll show you what they're for after,' Nora said, moving her and the chair beside the window and bringing a towel to drape around her shoulders. She combed out her tangled hair gently and walked round and round her, studying her head from all angles. 'Peyton, do you like Audrey Hepburn?'

'Better than anybody,' Peyton said. '*Breakfast at Tiffany's* is my favourite movie. I sat through it three times.'

'I did twice. You know what I think we'll do? I think we'll cut this hair into a kind of Audrey Hepburn cap. Very short and pixie-ish, a little curly. It would look wonderful with your features and your long neck. You game?'

'Yes,' Peyton whispered, with the sense of leaping blindly into a bottomless abyss.

She kept her eyes closed while Nora snipped and patted and studied. Somehow it was not like the ministrations of Mr Antoine. As she worked, Nora talked about her night in Atlanta.

'Well, first,' she said, as if Peyton had asked, 'I went to the movie. *La Strada*. Have you seen it?'

'No,' Peyton said, trying to imagine herself walking alone into an Atlanta movie theatre after dark.

'You've got to see it, kiddo. I'll take you to a matinée. OK, so then afterward I walked up the street to Buon Giorno's and had my clam linguine and a bottle of awful, wonderful Chianti. That's a red Italian wine, very raw and gutsy.'

'I know what it is,' said Peyton, who didn't.

'Well,' Nora continued, 'so then I went down to this little place by the bus station that has the best Dixieland jazz I have *ever* heard outside New Orleans. And I danced and whooped and hollered till about one, and then I came home.'

'By *yourself*?' Peyton squawked. 'Down by the *bus* station? Aunt Augusta would *die*!'

'Which is why we aren't going to tell her, isn't it?' Peyton could hear the smile in Nora's voice. 'Besides, I wasn't by myself. I went with somebody I met at Buon Giorno's. He knew about the place.'

'*He?*' Peyton's head was spinning with the enormity of it.

'A soldier who was eating his dinner alone. So I joined him. It's more fun to eat Italian *with* somebody. He was on his way to Fort Benning and had to catch a bus at two in the morning. So we figured we might as well hear some jazz before he left, and dance a little.'

'You picked up a soldier and went to the bus station?'

Aside from sitting down on a bare toilet seat in a public rest room, going to the bus station was the number-one taboo in Aunt Augusta's pantheon of crimes and misdemeanours. Prowling soldiers were unthinkable.

'For God's sake, Peyton, he was all of eighteen, and homesick for Tennessee. He was a sweet boy. You get so you can tell who's OK and who isn't. We had a wonderful time, and I kissed him goodbye and put him on a Trailways bus.'

Nora produced a bulbous hand-held hair dryer and aimed it at Peyton's head. Until the hot air hit her, Peyton did not realise that her neck was completely naked. She looked down. A mat of wiry hair lay on the floor under the chair.

'You cut it all off,' she wailed.

'Yep. Now look.'

Nora stepped back and Peyton looked. A thin deer of a girl with a short tousle of hair looked back. It was its own colour again, with tendrils framing her face. Something Nora had done to it made it shine softly, and it was somehow fuller than usual. It had curve and lift and bounce to it. The girl in the mirror was . . . interesting. Pretty? No, assuredly not. But for the first time in her life Peyton could see what she might look like as a woman.

Nora smiled down at her. She lifted one eyebrow: 'Well?'

'I . . . gee. I don't know. It isn't me, is it?'

'Yes, it is. It's you like you ought to be. That stuff on your head was like a dead muskrat lying up there. This sets you free. Now I can really see your father and your grandmother in you.'

Peyton, who had spent her entire life searching for signs of her mother in her undistinguished visage, felt something inside her lighten and lift, as if she had tossed out a heavy burden. At least she looked like *someone* now—if not her mother, then just maybe her mad, beautiful grandmother, her blade-featured father.

Her smile widened. 'Nobody at school has hair like this.'

'Precisely,' Nora said. 'Peyton, take it from one who knows. You aren't ever going to look like Brigitte Bardot or Jackie Kennedy. Don't waste your time wishing. Go with what you've got. It may not ring many bells at school, but I assure you there *is* a world beyond Lytton Grammar, and it's a lot more interesting. You're going to shine in that world like a star. Come on, kiddo, let's go try it out on somebody. Is your daddy in his office?'

'No! Not yet.'

'Chloe, then?'

'She's gone home. She works only half a day on Saturdays.'

'OK, your grandmother. I promised, anyway. Dump that afghan and put on some clothes. Your chariot awaits.'

Peyton tiptoed down the stairs to her room and put on a pair of slim blue pants and a white sweater she had got for Christmas and never worn. The sweater was too big, but somehow the drooping amplitude of it was all right with the long neck and the small shining head. She put on her sneakers and went hesitantly out into the kitchen.

'Miss Hepburn, as I live and breathe,' Nora said, smiling. She had changed into tight, faded blue jeans and a sweat shirt.

They dashed through the rain to the Thunderbird. Peyton scrunched herself into the passenger seat, loving the sleek, feral feeling of the car as it leapt away from the kerb and skimmed into flight.

Her grandmother was in the kitchen, stirring something in a pot. She heard them come in and turned from the stove. She looked first at Peyton, and a slow smile warmed her wild hawk's face. 'Well, here you are at last. I've waited a long time for you.'

Then she turned to Nora. 'It's nice to see you again,' she said, almost formally. 'Will you stay and have a cup of tea?'

They sat down before the blazing kitchen fireplace. Agnes McKenzie brought cups of the steaming brew and slices of seed cake almost shyly, as if offering them to royalty. She sat down then and sipped her own tea.

There was a silence. Finally Peyton could stand it no longer and said, 'How do you like my hair, Nana?'

Her grandmother studied her. 'You're not our little girl any more,' she said. 'But you're who you're going to be now, and that's a start. I can see the shape of you like a minnow in deep water. Or something in long grass. Something wild and shy, but the power's there. Oh, yes, it is. I always knew it would be.'

'Power?' Peyton said, appalled. She did not want power any more than she wanted wealth or celebrity. She would settle gratefully for the old anonymity, so long as no one laughed at her any more.

'Oh, yes. It'll be a long time until you grow into it, and it won't be any easy journey, but power.'

'Is it good power?' Nora said interestedly.

'It depends on who guides it,' Nana said. 'I plan to be on top of it like a duck on a june bug, but I'm not going to be able to go all the way with it.' Abruptly she got up from the table and said, 'Peyton, come on in the pantry with me. I need a load of firewood.'

Peyton rose to follow her grandmother.

Nora half rose, too. 'Won't you let me help?' she said. 'I don't want to feel like company.'

'But you are,' Agnes said, and smiled faintly at her, and went out of the kitchen with Peyton trailing behind her.

In the dim, cold little pantry she fished into the pocket of her apron, pulled something out and dropped it into Peyton's hand. Peyton looked down. It was a strange object, primitive and rather beautiful: an intricately woven knot that formed a rough cross on a leather thong.

'It's a special amulet. It protects you. I want you to put it on now, and I don't want you to take it off again.'

'Protects me against what?'

Her grandmother was silent, and then she said, 'I saw her again, your Cousin Nora. I saw her this morning when I built the fire.'

'The fire—that's not so good, is it? She wouldn't hurt me, Nana. I know she wouldn't. I don't think I like her very much, but she's always taking my side and doing things for me, and she absolutely hates Aunt Augusta. That can't be all bad, can it?'

Her grandmother shook her head impatiently. 'I can't see bad or good this time,' she said. 'I just know that I saw her first in the soup, and this time in the fire—I don't see bad; I don't see anything. It's like fog. I don't know what it means.'

Suddenly Peyton was tired of all of it—the dark pantry, the visions of fire and water. She wanted light, air, normalcy, laughter, the sound of her record player.

'I think we need to go, Nana,' she said. 'Daddy's going to be in before long and Nora's making Cuban black bean soup for supper.'

Her grandmother looked at her and sighed. 'So it begins,' she said. 'All right, Peyton. You run on and have your soup.'

AT SUPPER HER FATHER frankly stared at her. He said nothing, only nodded as Nora talked lazily about her trip to Atlanta the night before, and ate the rich, dark soup appreciatively and had another bowl, saying it made him feel as if he were at a real fiesta, and all the while Peyton was aware of his eyes on her.

Finally he said, 'I really like your hair, Peyton. I like the new clothes, too. You remember to thank your aunt, now.'

'She's going to hate the hair,' Peyton said.

Her father smiled, a small smile, but a smile nevertheless. 'I expect you're right,' he said. 'Never mind. This is good. She'll come around. Did you thank Nora for the haircut?'

'She did,' Nora said before Peyton could remember that she had not. 'We went down to her grandmother's afterward, to show her. I think she liked it, too.'

Her father looked at Peyton.

'She really did,' Peyton said, bending over her soup bowl.

'Well, then, you've got a hard row to hoe ahead of you,' Frazier said, but he smiled again. 'Nora, tell me where you learned to make this soup. Cuba, you said? Were you there long? I've always wanted to see Cuba.'

'It's a wonderful country,' Nora said. 'I might still be there if the revolution hadn't heated things up. I believe in it, but I don't want to live with it. I don't take easily to sacrifice and nobility.'

She smiled through smoke, and Peyton thought how plain she was, and yet how utterly arresting. It was hard to look away from her. She had brought out fat wax candles from somewhere, and painted wooden candlesticks, and they ate by the flickering light. In it, Nora looked like some impossible firebird that had alighted in a small southern town and decided to stay awhile, unaware that her plumage roiled the air around her. She wore a heavy cabled white turtleneck sweater and the black pants, and her long, thin hands weaved in and out of the candlelight as she talked of Cuba.

'I went there in nineteen fifty-two with a friend,' she said. 'I was just out of school and didn't know what I wanted to do, and I had always wanted to see Cuba. He had a motorcycle. We put it on a ferry and took off. He came back two months later. I stayed five years.'

Peyton saw her father remark the 'he', though he said nothing. It emboldened her to say, 'Why didn't your friend stay, too?'

'Tootie was a priest,' Nora said. 'He had to get back to his parish.'

'Tootie?' Peyton said.

'Tootie LeClerc, fresh out of Loyola in New Orleans. I met him on the beach in Miami and we spent the afternoon drinking beer. Once I saw the motorcycle and heard he was going to Cuba, I knew what my next move was going to be.'

'So you stayed on,' Frazier said.

'I did. At first I just wanted to be a tourist—we poked around Havana and did all the touristy things—but soon we both got restless. So we got on the motorcycle and headed west, toward Mariel. It's beautiful country, or it was then—wild and empty, with blue, blue water. And poor. That's where we began to see little adobe shacks with chickens going in and out of the open windows, and the village men hanging around the lone flyspecked cantina because one or another of the cement factories had shut down and there was no work. And the children, some naked, some in rags, playing in the roads with not a sign of any supervision, or a school anywhere. Tootie thought he'd found paradise; he went straight to the Catholic church and asked if he could sign on sans pay, and the old priest almost kissed him. I went into the cantina and told the barkeeper that I would start a little school for the children, teach them English and some geography and what all, in exchange for room and board in the village. I had a little money. I was going to stay until it ran out. So they found me a room with a village family and I moved in and fell in love with them and it and everything else, and when Tootie went back to New Orleans, I stayed. They were some of the great years of my life. It was as if that's what I was meant to be doing—living there with those people, teaching those children.'

'But you left,' Frazier McKenzie said.

'Things change. One day it was time. I came back to Miami and got a job with a programme they had for the Haitian refugees pouring into Florida from Papa Doc and his benevolent Tontons Macoute. But you don't want to hear all this.'

'I do,' he said. 'It's fascinating. Peyton and I both would love to hear your stories. You've done something really valuable.'

'One day I'll tell them all to you.' She smiled and got up and said, 'Leave the dishes. Peyton, come with me. I have something for you.'

The something was a tiny tiger kitten with slanted green eyes and a little spike of a tail. Nora brought his box out of the bathroom and set it down, and the kitten scrambled out onto the floor, mewling furiously. He looked at Peyton and she looked back.

'I found him behind a trash can at the bus station last night,' Nora said. 'Somebody had obviously dumped him. His name is Trailways, and he needs a friend.'

The kitten mewed again. Peyton put out a hand and he sniffed her fingers and then climbed into her lap and curled up. Something in her heart softened into a spreading pool. 'Is he for me?' she asked.

'If you want him. He'll need a lot of taking care of. Shots and most certainly a flea bath. We need to get a vet to check him.'

'Can I take him to my room?' Peyton said. Her voice was tight with love for the angry little cat.

'In a little while,' Nora said. 'You stay with him right now. I want to go down and tell your father about him. I get the idea that there haven't been many pets in this house.'

'Buddy had a dog, I think, but I don't remember it . . .'

'You just sit tight.' Nora got up and went down the stairs towards the breakfast room. Peyton wrapped a small towel around the kitten and took it and sat with it on the second step, out of sight but not out of hearing.

'. . . not set up here for a cat,' she heard her father say. 'Chloe isn't going to have time to take care of it when she gets tired of it.'

'She's not going to get tired of it, Frazier,' Nora said, and her voice was cool and utterly level. 'I wish you had seen her face.'

'Did you ever think of asking me first?'

'I did, and vetoed that idea in a second. Would you have permitted it? And besides, it isn't your kitten. It's Peyton's.'

There was more talk but the voices dropped and Peyton could not hear. She sat on the step and rocked the kitten against her.

Presently Nora came into the hall and looked up and made a circle with her thumb and forefinger. Peyton felt tears sting her eyes.

She slept that night with the susurration of the wind and rain in the trees outside and, just at her ear, the rusty purr of the kitten.

WHEN PEYTON WOKE on Sunday morning the house was still and full of pearly grey light, and the rain was a blanket of sound that muffled wakefulness. She was just putting an unwilling foot out from under her covers when she heard Chloe shriek from the kitchen.

Peyton was halfway into the kitchen before she remembered the kitten and registered that it was not in her bedroom. 'Oh, shit,' she said softly.

Chloe was standing, arms akimbo, in the middle of the kitchen, glaring down at her skirt. Trailways hung from it, fastened by his needlelike claws, swinging gently and lashing his meagre tail.

Peyton ran and unhooked him from Clothilde's skirt and folded him protectively into her arms, where he struggled and yowled.

'What that sorry thing doing in this house?' Chloe demanded. 'I was just standing here fixin' breakfast and he come barrelling out of your room and grab on my skirt before I even seen him.'

'I'm sorry, Chloe,' Peyton said miserably. 'I thought he was still with me. Nora brought him to me. His name is Trailways.'

'His name mud for all I care. Does your daddy know about him?'

'Yes. It's all right with him.'

'Well, if it get under my feet one more time I'm gon' stomp on it.'

'He won't,' Peyton said fervently. 'I'll keep him in my room. I'll feed him and clean up after him. He won't be a bit of trouble.'

Trailways stuck his sharp little head out of Peyton's arm and looked up into Chloe's face. He put out a tiny paw and patted her arm, seven or eight rapid, whisper-soft pats. 'Rowr?' he said.

Chloe's face struggled with implacability but lost. An unwilling grin broke its surface. 'Well, he's a feisty little thing, ain't he?'

'He's a good boy. You're going to love him, Chloe.'

'I ain't gon' love no flea-bitten stray cat. But maybe I ain't gon' hate him, either,' Clothilde said.

When Nora finally straggled down to breakfast, Peyton and her father were playing with Trailways, tossing a ball of kitchen twine for him. Peyton was laughing, and her father was smiling.

Peyton looked up as Nora came down the stairs and into the breakfast room. Instead of the dragon robe, she was wearing a short black sheath, a strand of pearls, and high-heeled black shoes. She had her hair pulled back into a chignon and had tied a red and black paisley silk scarf around it. She looked absolutely wonderful.

'I thought we'd be going to church,' Nora said. 'Am I too late? Is this wrong for church?'

'You look just fine,' Frazier said. 'You just took us by surprise. Here you are all dressed and Peyton's still in her pyjamas. I wasn't sure you'd want to go to church, but we're glad to have you.'

'I'd really like to. So, I see you've met Trailways,' Nora said. 'He's a cutie, isn't he?'

'He's not so bad. Where on earth did you find him?'

'Behind a garbage can at the restaurant,' Nora said easily. She smiled at Peyton. *We will always have our secrets, you and I*, the smile said. Peyton smiled back at her cousin. *Yes, secrets of our own, which nobody else will ever know,* her smile said back to Nora.

She went to dress, and Nora came into her room with her.

'Now. What are you going to wear to church?'

Without stopping for Peyton's answer, Nora went to her closet and opened the door. She shook her head a little and then reached in and pulled out the dress and jacket that Aunt Augusta had selected from the Tween Shop. They were just as bad as Peyton remembered.

'This?' Nora said.

'I hate it. It looks like a missionary-society dress.'

'Just you wait. Put it on and I'll be right back.'

Peyton slipped on the dark, sleeveless dress, which gaped and billowed on her, the skirt flapping at her calves, and she would not look into the mirror on her dressing table. There was no way anyone was going to get her into the Lytton First Methodist Church in this.

Nora came back with a shopping bag and began to spread things out on Peyton's bed. First she brought out safety pins and pinned the waist and armholes of the dress snugly. Then she took a big roll of two-sided tape and doubled the hem up and secured it with the tape. Peyton felt it just skimming her knees.

Nora clasped a string of irregular freshwater pearls around Peyton's neck, then she produced stockings and black suede shoes with low, shaped heels.

'Cuban heels,' she said. 'Do you think you can squinch your feet into them just for an hour?'

Peyton nodded, wondering how on earth she was going to walk.

'Now the jacket,' Nora said, and she slipped it over Peyton's arms and buttoned it at the throat, pulling out the pearls so that they lay just along the neckline. She puffed Peyton's hair, whisked on a bit of blusher and a slicking of lip gloss and stepped back.

'Wow,' she said. 'This is even better than I thought.'

Peyton minced over to the mirror in the too-tight heels, and looked. Holly Golightly did indeed look back, standing poised and straight, her stalk of a neck rising from the collar of her dress, her long legs graceful.

'I can't,' Peyton whispered. 'I can't wear this.'

'Oh, yes, you can, and you will,' Nora said, putting an arm around her shoulder. 'You're going to walk into that church with your father and me and you're going to hear a great big swoosh of breath from everybody there.'

'I'd hate that.'

'No, you wouldn't. Once you've heard it, you'll want to hear it everywhere you go.'

THERE WAS NO WHOOSH of indrawn breath as Peyton walked into the Methodist church, the church she had attended all her life. There was, however, a small silence from each pew as she passed, and then a little hum of conversation.

'Let me die,' Peyton whispered to the God who never seemed to hear her, and she slipped into the McKenzie pew. When she turned to seat herself, she looked back. Everywhere she looked, there were smiles. Her Uncle Charles held up his thumb and forefinger in an OK sign. Only Aunt Augusta was not smiling. She looked as if she had swallowed something rancid.

The sermon seemed interminable. When it ended, Peyton stifled an urge to dash out the back entrance, and trotted dumbly up the aisle behind her father. Nora walked ahead of them, head high, a small smile on her mouth. Peyton thought that there had been nothing like her in this church in its living memory, though Nora wore plain black, like half the women there, and pearls, and just the silk scarf. Still, eyes tracked her, heads went together, a soft babble rose wherever she passed. When the eyes turned to Peyton the babble swelled. Finally, the three of them gained the cold freedom of the porch, and then they were in the car.

'You ladies surely kicked up a fuss,' her father said. 'I never saw so much whispering and eye-rolling and what-all. I thought for a minute they were going to clap.'

Suddenly Peyton was wild to be home, to skin out of the

pinned-up clothes, to curl up with Trailways under her afghan and read away the long afternoon.

'Augusta has asked us to lunch,' her father said. 'I thought we'd go and get it over with. If we don't, she's going to be at the house every morning until she finds out all she wants to know about Nora.'

'*Daddy*,' Peyton wailed.

'It's not for long, Peyton. And it's been a while since you've seen your Uncle Charlie. I want Nora to meet him.'

'I look forward to it,' Nora murmured.

Augusta McKenzie met them at the doorway of her home, a rambling brick ranch-style structure with black shutters and a path bordered with azalea bushes.

Augusta kissed Frazier lightly on the cheek and nodded to Nora.

'Your new clothes suit you very well, Peyton,' she said. 'I'm sorry you didn't think so much of your pretty permanent. Did your Cousin Nora cut it for you?'

The smile she bent on Nora was sharklike and brief.

'Yes, I did,' Nora said sweetly. 'We thought something a little simpler, maybe. I don't think Peyton quite knew how to take care of the permanent. I know she appreciated it, though.'

'I'm sure,' Augusta said.

She led them into her living room, done in turquoise and rose and beetling with bulbous brocade pieces. Charles McKenzie was perched uncomfortably on a wing chair, stiff in a blue suit and a red and blue tie. He clashed with the room.

Charles was a squashed and spread version of his older brother. You could see the resemblance in the grey eyes and dark hair, but the rest seemed blurred and sagging like a melting snowman. His nose was traced with red veins, he had two shiny-shaved chins poised over his starched collar, and his stomach pushed unhappily over his belt. Except on Sundays, Peyton could not remember ever seeing him in anything but hunting boots or desiccated old moccasins. She loved him. When she was very small, he used to toss her in the air and catch her, and she remembered her shrieks of joy.

He got up and hugged her briefly. He smelt as he always did, of whiskey and cigar smoke and his aftershave and, somehow, of the hunting dogs he kept over at Chief Fletcher's house.

'You look mighty pretty, honey,' he said. 'All grown up.'

'This is Peyton's cousin, Nora Findlay,' her father said, and Nora put out her hand, smiling. Uncle Charlie took it, reddening.

'I'm glad to meet you finally,' Nora said.

'Pleasedtomeecha,' Charles McKenzie mumbled.

'Please sit down,' Aunt Augusta said. 'Lunch will be only a minute. Now, Nora, tell us all about yourself. I knew your Lytton cousin, Lila Lee, for ever, of course, but I don't believe I ever met her Cousin Carolyn. Your mother. She's passed away, I understand?'

'Yes, she has,' Nora said. Peyton knew that Aunt Augusta knew that. She knew also that Nora knew she knew. Her stomach knotted, but Nora only said, 'As you know, she was sick for a long time before she died. I don't remember much about my father. So the only family I can come close to claiming is here in Lytton.'

'And you'll be moving on to a job in Atlanta, you said?'

'Well, actually . . .'

'I hope Nora will be staying awhile with us, Augusta,' Frazier McKenzie said. 'There are plans for a new joint English class with Lytton and Carver Highs, and I've suggested Nora for it. We'll know this week, but I'd say it was a done deal.'

'Well, Nora, you've landed well, haven't you?' Augusta said. And then, 'I think I heard Doreen say lunch was ready. Let's go on in.'

Aunt Augusta's table was spread with linen and china and crystal and silver, most of it in turquoise and rose. A prim tower of artificial fruit rose from a silver epergne in the middle of the table. Rose candles burned on either side of it.

'My goodness, it looks like a wedding with the candles and all,' Nora said. 'Beautiful, Aunt Augusta. Or should I say "Cousin"?'

'"Augusta" will do,' Peyton's aunt said. 'You're a bit too old to be my niece, and we're really not cousins. Thank you. I thought the candles because it's so dreary outside.'

A young black girl came into the dining room carrying a tureen. She wore a black dress and a starched white apron.

Peyton stared. 'Doreen! What are you doing in that thing?'

Doreen was the grandniece of Clothilde, a quiet girl only a few years older than Peyton. Her mother had died when she was small, and she did not know who her father was. Chloe looked after her and her younger brother, Tyrone. Peyton had played in the woods with both of them all through her childhood.

Doreen grinned but did not move her eyes from the tureen. She set it down in the middle of the table, where it slopped a bit of soup onto the tablecloth.

'Towel, please, Doreen,' Aunt Augusta said evenly, and when the girl had left the room she added, 'I'll never get her properly trained to serve. But she's helpful with the cleaning.'

'What's she doing in that apron thing?' Peyton asked curiously.

'For heaven's sake, Peyton, it's what people's maids wear,' her aunt said. 'Just because Chloe comes to work looking like a rag-picker does not mean it's proper. I bought the uniform for Doreen because I want her to learn how to be a good maid. She didn't go to school past the third grade because she had to look after Tyrone, and at least she can always find work if she's trained.'

No one spoke. Doreen came back into the room with a towel, looking as though she would burst into tears. Nora leaned towards her and took the towel. 'Let me,' she said. 'It's easier to reach from here. No, wait a minute, Doreen, don't go yet. I'm Nora Findlay, Peyton's cousin.'

Doreen looked at her wildly.

Nora smiled and said, 'You're a good maid, Doreen, but I wonder if you might not like to go back to school?'

'No'm,' the girl said, casting a look at Aunt Augusta. 'I've missed too much now. This is fine.'

'Well, look. I'm starting a special English class at Carver. You might enjoy sitting in sometime, when you're done with your work, of course. And I do tutoring, too. We could catch you up.'

'That will do, Doreen,' Aunt Augusta said, and the girl fled.

Augusta turned to Nora. 'It may not be the custom in some of the places you've lived,' she said tightly, 'but in Lytton people do not steal one another's maids.'

'I wasn't stealing her, I was emancipating her,' Nora said, and there were two round spots of colour high on her cheekbones. 'It was a notion Mr Lincoln had, a long time ago. I thought perhaps you'd heard of it.'

'You may bring in the plates, Doreen,' Augusta called. The girl did, and handed them round. The table was silent.

The meal was heavy and not particularly good, and it seemed to go on for years.

When at last it was over, they went back into the living room, and then Charles McKenzie said, 'Got a new shotgun the other day, Frazier. It's out in the garage. Want to go have a look?'

'Charles, let Frazier sit and digest his lunch,' Aunt Augusta snapped.

Nora stood up. 'I would love to see it, Charles,' she said. 'I learned skeet and trap shooting when I was in Cuba. I'm a pretty good shot, if I do say so. Will you show me?'

Charles McKenzie's ears reddened. He had no choice. He got up and shambled out of the room. Nora followed him.

After they left, the silence seemed to swell and shimmer. Even Peyton knew that what Nora had done had crossed some sort of boundary, though she did not know what it was. Aunt Augusta's eyes were almost popping out of her rosy face. Peyton knew, too, that whatever it was she was bursting to spill would not come forth while she was in the room.

'Aunt Augusta, may I go in the den and listen to the radio?' she said.

'Of course, Peyton. You might want to close the door so we don't disturb each other.'

Peyton got up and wobbled on Nora's heels into the den, where the radio had been banished when the new Motorola TV was given pride of place in the living room. The den had started life as a small screened porch and was barely large enough to accommodate the radio and two battered Leatherette recliners. It smelt of cigars and, faintly, of sweet bourbon whiskey. Peyton turned on the radio and closed the glass French doors that separated the den from the living room. She then kicked off her shoes and curled up on the floor next to the big radio and laid her cheek against its fretwork as she had when she was a child, feeling the warmth and the living vibration from the station in Atlanta seep into her like sun. She must have slept. The next thing she knew someone had opened the glass doors and she could hear her father saying, 'Well, it's been a treat as usual, Augusta, but we've got to be on our way. I don't think Peyton has done her homework yet.'

Nora and Uncle Charles stood at the door, laughing.

'Thank you, Charles,' Nora said, her rich voice lilting with pleasure. 'What a lovely way to spend a rainy afternoon. Maybe you'll let me shoot it one day. I don't hunt, but I'm a terrific shot.'

Uncle Charles said heartily, 'It would be my pleasure.' Then he looked at Aunt Augusta's face and dropped his eyes to study his shoes.

'Thank you, Augusta,' Nora said, kissing Augusta on the cheek; Augusta flinched as if she had been bitten by a blue-tail fly. 'It was a wonderful lunch. Your house is just extraordinary.'

Peyton ran with Nora through the rain to the car. Behind them, they heard Augusta saying to Frazier, 'How can you possibly think she can stay in your house? I smelt whiskey on her breath, Frazier. Surely that should be enough for you.'

Nora laughed and shook out her wet copper hair. 'A little shot of Uncle Charles's stash wouldn't hurt her any,' she said.

Peyton was silent. In her world, no living white woman had ever been known to drink anything but eggnog at Christmas and a glass of champagne at weddings.

Her father was quiet on the drive home, and as they were putting away their wet things, he said, 'I've got a good bit of work to do. I'll be out in my office for a while.'

Peyton looked after him as he left the kitchen. Sunday afternoon was always their time to drive up to the Howard Johnson's on the interstate and have ice cream, and afterwards to watch television. Peyton had never known her father to work on Sunday afternoons.

Nora looked after him thoughtfully, then said, 'Get Trailways and I'll show you some of the things I brought with me from Cuba.'

'I think I'll read,' Peyton said. Tears were smarting in her eyes.

'This is better than any book,' Nora said, ruffling her hair. 'I'll even show you my voodoo charms. No one has seen them before.'

Peyton brought Trailways to Nora's room and settled down in the middle of her unmade bed. The kitten burrowed under the bedclothes and down to the bottom of the bed, scrabbling furiously, then curled into a ball, and started purring loudly.

Nora opened a big box that had been tied with twine and pulled out her treasures for Peyton's delectation. There were bolts of vivid, printed cloth—batik, Nora said. Big, bursting scrapbooks, too, came out of the trunk—'I'll show you some day'—and an ornate cigar box holding what Nora called her voodoo charms, which were small carved figures, bound clumps of feathers, mirrors, and a chicken's foot.

'Yuck,' Peyton said.

'Yeah, well, it's got power, no matter how it looks,' Nora said. 'Chickens are powerful carriers in voodoo. This chicken foot will protect you from were-tigers. That's probably why you never see them in the South—all those chickens.'

Peyton grinned unwillingly. The hurt of her father's defection eased slightly. 'What's that?' she asked, looking at a beautifully carved ebony box with a lock. It looked very old.

'That's my private stuff,' Nora said. 'The things that only I see. Photos, my journal, letters . . . Do you keep a journal, Peyton?'

'No,' Peyton said, suddenly on fire to open the box and let Nora's secrets fly out into the room like Pandora's furies.

'Well, that's one thing you simply have to do,' Nora said. 'How will you know what you think if you don't write it down? How will you remember who you were? I'm going to get you a good leather one next time I'm in Atlanta.'

Dusk was falling outside. The rain had stopped, and long, stabbing rays of brilliant red sun were piercing the clouds.

'Look at that. Red as sin,' Nora said. 'Does your father usually come in for dinner? If he doesn't, I'll fix us something.'

'He always does,' Peyton said, the pain welling back. 'Always. I don't know why he's acting like this.'

Nora was silent for a moment and then said, 'I do. He's mad at me. I think I shouldn't have gone out to the garage with your Uncle Charles, though God knows what your father and your aunt thought we were doing out there. You stay here and look through this stuff, if you want to. I'm going out there to talk to him.'

She pulled a sweatshirt over her thin T-shirt and padded out of the room, in her soft moccasins. Peyton sat still on the bed for a time after she left. Then she got up and went down the stairs and out of the back door to the foot of the stairs that led up to her father's office over the garage. She had no compunction about eavesdropping. This was about her, too.

'. . . if I've broken any of the house rules, I'm sorry, Frazier,' Nora was saying. 'But you'll have to tell me what they are. I can't read your mind, and I'd hate to have you running out here every time I cross some border I don't know is there.'

'I don't want to set rules for you, Nora,' her father said evenly. 'But I should think it would be apparent that young women don't go off with men and come back smelling like whiskey.'

'Maybe not in Lytton,' Nora said. 'But they do in the places I've lived, Frazier. In those places, it's an honour to be shown someone's treasures. Couldn't you see how proud Charles was of that shotgun? He wanted somebody to see it. And yes, I did have one drink with him. In the Latin countries, it's an insult to refuse someone's hospitality.'

'You're in a small southern town now, Nora. There's nothing Latin about it.'

'Nothing Latin in Lytton,' Nora said, and Peyton could hear laughter in her voice. 'No, there certainly isn't. But, Frazier, don't you see what she's made of him? He's like a ghost afraid to haunt his own house. How can a woman do that to a man? I wanted to give him back something . . .'

'Nora, I'm glad you're here. I thought it was a good idea and I still do. But there are some things that I just can't have Peyton learning.'

'What? Like racism? Like the fine art of inflicting humiliation?'

'Nora—'

'Frazier, your daughter is withering before she even blooms. She knows nothing, expects nothing. She doesn't even know how to laugh, as far as I can see. It breaks my heart. It may well be that I'm not the right person to teach her, but someone must do it besides Augusta. I've spent a long time finding out the way I want to live, and if I'm not free to live that way I just can't stay. I can accommodate some of your rules, of course, but, if I do, you'll have to accommodate some of my un-Lyttonly notions. But first we have to be able to talk. If you find you just can't do that, then I'll find another place to live. But I have to know what your . . . rules for living are.'

'I guess I just never thought about it,' her father said.

'Then how on earth do you know who you are?'

Abruptly the door leading to the landing opened, and Nora stepped out into the dusk. Peyton ducked behind the big camellia bush that sheltered the side of the garage. After Nora went into the house, she crept out and tiptoed through the kitchen and into her small room. She curled herself under her afghan.

Later—much later, it seemed—she heard her father come into the living room and click on the television set.

'Anybody want some supper?' he called. 'All of a sudden I feel like Howard Johnson's fried clams. Have I got any takers?'

She heard Nora's step coming down the stairs, and her voice answering. Peyton skinned out of bed and into her jeans and a sweater, light flooding back as if it had never been dark.

5

The next morning Nora said at breakfast that she planned to spend the day getting to know the inside of Lytton.

'What inside?' Peyton said, feeding the clamouring Trailways bits of her bacon under the table.

'You know, the insides of places and the people who run them. The library. The bank. The luncheonette. Who knows? Maybe the pool hall and the barbershop.'

'People are going to talk about you if you go in the pool hall and the barbershop,' Peyton said.

'People already are,' Nora said, smiling. 'Your aunt undoubtedly had the jungle drums going about my little fling with your uncle before the door was closed behind us.'

'Don't you care?'

Nora blew smoke. 'No. I don't give a tinker's damn about what most people think about me; I stopped that a long time ago. Now I only care about a very few. You. Your daddy. Chloe. Your grandmother. And that about does it.'

Chloe came in with fresh biscuits and placed them on the table. She turned to Nora. 'Doreen told me you said you might teach her a little bit. I sho' would appreciate that. Maybe just enough to read better. She could go to high-school classes at night up to College Park if she could read better. She's a real bright girl. She don't need to be a maid the rest of her life. '

'I'd love to,' Nora said. 'Let me get a week or so of my new job under my belt—if I get it, of course—and then we'll set something up. But you better tell her not to tell Mrs McKenzie. She's already accused me of maid rustling.'

THAT MORNING at school Miss Carruthers said, in front of the entire class, 'Peyton, you look very nice with your new haircut. Very chic.'

After that no one said a word about her hair.

She took Trailways with her to the Losers Club that afternoon, and had to carry him in Chloe's lidded sewing basket because he writhed and howled so. When she got to the shed behind the parsonage, Boot and Ernie were waiting.

'What you got in that basket?' Boot said.

'A king cobra, at the very least,' Ernie said sourly.

'Never heard of no cobra spit like a cat.' Boot grinned. 'Come on, Peyton, let's see him. Mamaw told me about him.'

Peyton opened the basket and Trailways leapt out. He stood glaring at them, his little bowed legs planted apart, his spiky tail quivering. Then he found himself a spot on the frayed rug in front of the space heater and settled into a ball of sleep.

Ernie was heating water for instant cocoa. 'Cats make me

sneeze,' he said. 'He can't stay very long, Peyton.'

'He's a special cat,' Peyton said. 'My Cousin Nora went up to Atlanta for dinner and met some soldier, and they were at the Trailways bus station and she saw him behind a garbage can. She brought him home to me. Trailways is his name.'

'What she doin' hanging around that bus station?' Boot said, scandalised.

'It figures,' Ernie said prissily.

'She wasn't hanging around it,' Peyton retorted. 'She was only there to drop off the soldier. He was on his way to Fort Benning, and anyway, he was only about eighteen. Nora met him in the restaurant where she had dinner. An Italian restaurant.'

She cut her eyes at Ernie and Boot to see how her cousin's lone dinner in Atlanta was being received. They were silent.

'They went to a jazz place and danced after that,' she added. 'She's going to take me with her to Atlanta next time she goes.'

'Man, that is *something*!' Boot said. 'When y'all going?'

'Probably next weekend. We're going to spend the day.'

'Well, you and your new haircut have got a full social schedule,' Ernie drawled. It was the first time he had mentioned her haircut.

Peyton looked at him. 'Nora cut it,' she said.

'It's quite pretty, if you like that kind of thing,' Ernie said, stirring hot water into three paper cups.

'Everybody thinks it looks like Audrey Hepburn's,' Peyton said.

'More like Aldo Ray's. But never mind me. If your cousin did it, it must be holy.'

They were silent again for a while, sipping the cocoa, and then Ernie said, 'I'm going to suspend the club for a while. Nobody's heart seems to be in it, and I've got better things to do.'

'Naw,' Boot cried. 'My heart is in it good!'

'Peyton's isn't. She's all tied up with her sainted cousin.'

Fear flooded Peyton. Not to have the Losers Club . . .

'No, I'm not,' she said. 'I'm not going to do things with her much. She's dumb. She does crazy things. And everybody's going to be talking about us because of her. She's made Aunt Augusta mad as a wet hen. She went out to the garage with Uncle Charlie yesterday, and came back smelling like whiskey. Isn't that just the pits?'

'Everybody knows about that,' Ernie said.

'See why I don't like her?' Peyton said, close to tears.

'It doesn't sound to me like you don't like her,' Ernie said.

'What if I brought her one afternoon?' she said desperately. 'You'd see for yourself how awful she is.'

'You know we said we'd never let outsiders in here,' Ernie said.

'She wouldn't have to come more than once, Ernie, just so you could realise why I'm not going to get tied up with her. Besides, she might fit right in. She does the most awful, embarrassing things . . .'

'I'll have to think about it,' Ernie said, and the conversation gradually faded and died. Presently Peyton picked up Trailways and stuffed him back into the basket and went home with him.

Nora came in pink-cheeked and windblown from her day around the town and went upstairs. She did not put her head into Peyton's room, and Peyton did not climb the stairs to hers. From now on, she thought, she was going to exclude her cousin from her life. The club; oh, she could not let the club go, not yet . . .

That night, Nora wore a white cashmere sweater and grey flannel slacks to dinner. The candlelight gave her face a deeper glow and lit her hair to what Peyton fancied, having lately read Tennyson, was titian red. Chloe had made her famous vegetable beef soup and cornbread before she left, and there was an apple pie warm on the stove.

'Perfect for a cold night,' her father said, sliding into his seat. 'We're not done with winter yet, I don't think. You girls look mighty pretty, or is it the candlelight?'

They were back in the little breakfast room off the kitchen, but Nora had brought in the wooden candlesticks and lit the candles.

'I had a call from the chairman of the Fulton County Board today, Nora,' Frazier said. 'Everybody thinks the idea is a good one. We can't offer you much in the way of a salary, but I think that could be negotiated if we do the class more than one semester. I'd be pleased if you'd accept. I know Peyton would, too.'

Peyton dropped her eyes. 'Yes,' she mumbled.

'We wouldn't start for a week or so, but as it happens we need a substitute in sophomore English on Thursday and Friday. Mrs Camp is going to see her daughter's new baby.'

'I'd love to substitute,' Nora said. 'I'll get her lesson plans tomorrow, or if she'd rather, we could do a book-discussion group. I've had other sophomores who liked that.'

'I think at this point she'd be grateful if you'd simply sit there and keep them quiet,' Frazier said. 'She's been trying to get away to see her grandchild for two months now. I think the book discussion sounds interesting. Why don't you try it? Give you an idea of how your class will work.'

'I will, then. In fact, I think I'll use *To Kill a Mockingbird* for my book discussion and first class.' She turned to Peyton. 'You've read *To Kill a Mockingbird*, haven't you?'

Peyton shook her head.

'Well, then, that's our first priority. It catches the small-town South better than anything I've ever read, and it says some things about the South that need to be said.'

'Like what?'

'You'll see.'

NORA MET her substitute English class on Thursday morning, and by lunchtime it had passed into legend. Word leapt from Lytton High to Lytton Grammar like wildfire, and Peyton, eating her sandwich and reading *Little Women* alone in the lunchroom, looked up to find herself encircled by other students.

'Hear your cousin's over at the high school teaching nigger stuff,' Wesley Cato said. Wesley was fifteen and had repeated the seventh grade three times. Peyton merely looked at him.

'She's reading some kind of book about a nigger who raped a white girl and got shot by the police,' LeeAnne McGahee said. LeeAnne was twelve and looked eighteen, and was much admired for her immobile blonde bouffant and her projectile breasts.

'That's *To Kill a Mockingbird*,' Peyton said loftily. 'It's won all kinds of prizes. Nora gave it to me to read but I haven't yet.'

They stared at her, uncertain after this unexpected reaction.

'Well, it must be good if they shot the nigger,' Wesley said.

'It's about intolerance and prejudice in a little southern town,' Peyton said. 'You really ought to like it, Wesley.'

'I hear there's a retard in it, too,' LeeAnne said.

'Yep. So you'd like it, too.'

Shorn of their weapons, they smirked at her and sidled away. Peyton's heart was hammering in her chest, but she was also elated. She had stood down two of Lytton Grammar's most treasured icons and had come out the better for it. A flame of pure power leapt in her blood.

Maybe that's the power Nana was talking about, she thought. Maybe I have power in my words.

By the end of the day the rumours were a conflagration. Nora Findlay was reading tenth-graders a story about niggers raping people and about other people killing them. And it was the gospel truth that three of the boys—football players all, repeating the tenth grade for the second time—had offered in graphic terms to service Nora right there on her desk, and she had looked at them and laughed and said, 'Not on your best day, you horny little bastards,' whereupon the rest of the class had broken into cheers. And it was also gospel that when the class was over, she had walked out lighting a cigarette, and looked back and grinned and made a circle of her thumb and forefinger at the remaining students in the classroom. The entire student body of Lytton Grammar School was buzzing with Nora.

'But when the principal stuck his head in to see how she was doing, she just smiled and said, "Fine, sir. You have nice students here," and he like to busted his face smiling back,' a student told Peyton on the school steps. 'My brother said that after he'd gone she just looked at the class and winked. He said everybody hoped nobody tells on her. They thought she was great.'

Peyton knew that nobody would tell parents or faculty about Nora Findlay. She was life, rebellion, even affirmation to them. No teacher had ever been anything but the oppressor. They would simply say, 'Oh, just fine, thanks. She's nice,' to their parents, and the faculty would say to each other what a sweet girl she seemed to be, so deferential to the older ones.

Peyton did not think it could last, of course; Nora was bound to be found out in this small, airless arena. But for now she was flying high, and Peyton soared with her. One of the cheerleaders actually asked her to sit with them at lunch the next day.

'I'm going home, thanks,' Peyton said. 'My cousin and I always have lunch together.'

That evening as they sat at dinner Frazier McKenzie said, 'Well, how did it go at the high school today?'

'Just fine,' Nora said. 'Peyton, please pass the butter.'

PEYTON WENT BACK to the Losers Club the next afternoon, expecting it would be a triumph to have a cousin who had embarrassed her in front of the entire town.

But Ernie and Boot said nothing about Nora.

'I'm reading *To Kill a Mockingbird*,' Peyton said, trying to sound offhand. 'Nora gave me a copy. She's teaching it to her class, too.'

'A nice little book,' Ernie said. 'Not, of course, the great American novel, but nice.'

'That idiot,' Nora said, grinning, when Peyton told her that night what Ernie had said. 'That's just what it is.'

On Saturday morning they went to Atlanta. The fresh cold had given way before the green surf of spring rolling north from Florida, and the earth smelt wet and new and rich. The sun was mild.

'If you'll put on your sweater we'll put the top down,' Nora said. 'I'll turn the heater on. I used to do that all the time in the winter in Miami, whenever it got a little chilly. There's nothing like spring wind in your face and warm air on your feet.'

And there wasn't. By the time the little pink car rolled into downtown Atlanta, Peyton was drunk on air and light and wind and warm feet.

'We'll park at Rich's because it's a good starting place. But I assume you don't want to go in,' Nora said.

'Never again.'

'Never say never.'

They walked up Peachtree Street from Rich's in the spring sun.

The streets were full of people moving languidly.

'This is nice,' Nora said. 'This reminds me of a Saturday afternoon in Havana. Everybody came out into the streets.'

'To do what?' Peyton asked.

'Just to be there,' Nora said. 'You need to learn the fine art of just being, Peyton. I don't think your daddy or your Aunt Augusta is going to teach you that, so I guess the job falls to me. The first thing you do when you're being is to kind of float around seeing what you can see. Listen hard. Smell the smells—like that peanut shop over there. And the narcissus and daffodils from that lady on the corner.'

Peyton slowed down, consciously slackened her muscles, and sniffed the air. It's Atlanta in the spring, she thought in surprise. I'll never forget it. I'd know it anywhere. It's not like any other smell.

They stopped at a little stationery store in the Peachtree Arcade, a wondrous hall between two buildings, two storeys high, completely arched over with glass. The arcade was full of people, milling and chattering and examining wares spread out on tables. They did not look, to Peyton's eyes, very prosperous. This was just the sort of place Aunt Augusta was always warning her about. Not as bad as the bus station, but in the same arena.

'*Exactly* like Havana,' Nora said. 'Wonderful.'

In a far corner of the shop there was a dusty pile of old books. All were leather and some were stamped with faded gold. Nora riffled through them, smiling appreciatively. 'Lovely,' she said. 'Whole lives, right here in these books. What do you think of this one, Peyton?' She held up a green, soft-leather book, faded to a pale sage. Inside, in a faint copperplate hand, was written on the flyleaf, *Anna Marjorie Stephens. Her book*. There had been a date, but it was lost now. The thick ivory pages were edged with dull gold. Some of the first pages had been torn out, but the rest were blank and ruled with sepia ink.

'Do you like this? I think it's gorgeous,' Nora said. 'You'd always have Anna Marjorie looking over your shoulder, wouldn't you? She'd be the only one you'd have to share your secret thoughts with.'

'It's pretty,' Peyton said dutifully. She had thought they would go to the Cokesbury Book Shop and select a proper diary. A new one.

'I think you should have it,' Nora said. 'When you're grown and you look back over this, you'll see that there's a resonance to it that a mass-produced teenager's diary could never have.'

She paid for the book and they went out into the street. 'I guess it's about lunchtime,' Nora said. 'There's a delicatessen over there. Have you ever had a pastrami on rye?'

'I don't think so,' Peyton said faintly.

'Well, then, come on,' Nora said, starting towards the big delicatessen across from the arcade. 'Best in the world. But I expect they could rustle you up a hamburger if you'd like.'

When they approached the deli they saw a crowd on the sidewalk. People were milling about, buzzing angrily, and there were policemen with nightsticks.

'They must hate the day's special,' Nora said, pushing through to look in the window. Then she said, 'Look, Peyton, it's a sit-in. See those black kids at the counter? There's no food in front of them and not a living soul at the entire counter. Looks like we'd have our choice of seats.'

'Are we going in there?' Peyton squeaked. She knew that people went to jail for sitting in. Why, she could not quite remember.

'I thought we might.'

'Will we get arrested?'

'Oh, no. It's OK for us to eat in there. Just not them.'

'Is it against the law? Will they be arrested?'

'Probably not, unless they start a fuss. Sit-ins are a nonviolent protest. But the restaurant owner gets to decide if he'll serve Negroes or not. Obviously this one doesn't.'

'I can't go in there, Nora. There's a television camera over there. What if Daddy and Aunt Augusta saw me on TV?'

'I hope they'd be proud of you. Come on, Peyton. Sometimes it's necessary to do something that scares you. I think this is one of those times.'

They went inside. There was a faint garlicky smell and stratas of cigarette smoke hung in the air. Behind the counter, two red-faced waitresses were sitting on stools and staring out of the window.

Nora sauntered to the counter and sat down beside one of the young Negroes. He looked at Nora, who smiled. Tentatively he smiled back. The other three men looked over, and nodded.

'What's good here?' Nora asked.

'I don't think we're likely to find out,' said the first young man.

Nora nodded thoughtfully. Then she raised her voice slightly and said, 'Miss? My cousin and I would like to order some lunch.'

'We don't serve Negroes,' the waitress said tightly.

'Well, we shouldn't have any trouble, then, should we? I think we'd both like a hamburger, and pickles and coleslaw on the side, and a coffee for me and Coca-Cola for the young lady.'

The woman stared 'You may not be Negroes, but you're sitting with them,' she said. 'I'm not going to serve you.'

'I thought this was a public restaurant,' Nora said mildly. 'If that's not the case, I think that guy out there with the television camera is just waiting to know about it.'

'The owner won't let the newspeople in,' the woman said.

'Now I really don't believe that's legal. That guy out there would be real surprised to find that you all hadn't heard of the Constitution.'

A bald man put his head round a door at the end of the counter.

'She's threatening to bring the TV in here if we don't serve her,' the waitress squealed.

'Then serve the bitch,' he shouted, and shut the door.

'All right. What was it, hamburgers?' the waitress snapped.

'Yes. Six. With six sides of pickles and coleslaw and five coffees and a Coca-Cola.'

'Mr Stern!' the waitress shrieked.

'Do it,' he snarled from behind the door. 'Do it and get that trash out of my place.'

When the hamburgers came, they all ate silently and neatly. Peyton's face was burning. When they had finished and Nora picked up the bill, the first young man said, 'Thank you. We were getting pretty hungry. I hope we didn't scare the young lady.'

'I wasn't scared,' said Peyton, surprising herself.

They pushed through the crowd outside. 'What's going on in there?' asked a reporter. A cameraman started filming. Peyton sidled behind Nora, who merely smiled.

'Absolutely nothing,' she said. 'Just some people having lunch.'

They walked back to the parking garage in silence, the afternoon shading towards dusk. Peyton realised that she was trembling.

When the car came, Nora said, 'You still up for an early dinner? Or do you just want to go home? By the way, Peyton, I'm proud of you.'

'I'm still a little hungry,' Peyton lied. 'I'm really in the mood for some Italian food.'

'You got it,' Nora said, smiling, and she turned the car north up Peachtree Street.

'ARE YOU GOING to tell him?' Peyton asked later as Nora swung the car to the kerb in front of their house.

'Tell him what?'

'Any of it. You know. The sit-in and all that stuff. That I drank wine.'

'You didn't drink enough wine to make a chicken blink. It's a sin to eat ravioli without wine. No. I'm not going to tell him, unless you do first. I won't lie, but I won't tell him, either. That's for you to decide.'

'I don't think I will,' Peyton said. The day hung glittering like a Christmas ornament in her mind.

'Good. Everybody ought to have one or two private things.'

The house was dark. It was still early, but her father often went to bed early and read. Peyton's muscles relaxed slightly. It would not be required of her, then, to share this perfect day and night.

They tiptoed inside, and a light went on in the kitchen.

'Oh, shit,' Nora said softly.

Frazier McKenzie came into the room. He was still dressed, wearing his tan Perry Como cardigan, tweed trousers and house slippers. His face was remote. Peyton knew he was displeased.

He said nothing, merely looked at Nora. She, too, was silent, only smiling a little.

Peyton heard her voice spilling out of her like a broken water main: 'Oh, Daddy, it was just wonderful! Nora bought me a journal in the Peachtree Arcade and then we rode through Buckhead—you should see the houses there, Daddy, they're mansions—and then we went to this Italian place and I had ravioli, it's like these little pouches with sausage in them and sauce on them—'

She stopped and looked up at him.

His face remained closed and still, and then he smiled. 'You had a big day, didn't you?' he said.

'Oh, yes,' Peyton breathed in relief and exultation.

'It *was* a good day,' Nora said. 'Maybe next time you'll come with us.'

'Maybe I will,' he said.

THAT NIGHT, Peyton wrote in her diary. She sat cross-legged on her bed, Trailways snugged into the curve of her thigh, and stared at the blank first page. I have no idea how to write in a diary, she thought.

'It's just for you,' Nora's voice repeated in her head. 'Nobody will ever see it unless you show it to them. Write anything you want to. Write who you hate and who you love. What you're reading. What Trailways looks like when he lies in that patch of sunlight on the dining-room table. The whole point is to have a record of how you really were at twelve going on thirteen. I can promise you you're not going to remember yourself that way. It'll be good to be able to look back and check in with the real Peyton McKenzie *circa* nineteen sixty-one.'

Tentatively, Peyton wrote the date and then: *Today I went into Atlanta with my Cousin Nora. We had lunch at a delicatessen and dinner at an Italian restaurant. I had ravioli and Chianti wine. It was good. We sang Nora's college songs on the way home. I thought Daddy would be mad, but he wasn't.*

She stopped, and then she wrote: *I was at a sit-in. There wasn't much to it but I think I'm glad I did it. It's very late and Trailways looks like a pile of feathers from a chicken. I can feel his purr all the way up my leg and into my chest. Goodbye. Peyton McKenzie.*

NORA'S FIRST EXPERIMENTAL English class was held the following Monday at Carver High, the black school literally across the railroad tracks from the main body of Lytton. It consisted of honours English students from both high schools, grades ten through twelve. It was held at Carver because the school board thought it only courteous for the white school to make the first visit.

The class was scheduled for ten in the morning. By noon the news of it was scattering through the grammar school like spilt mercury. Jerry Mooney, the massive, truculent captain of the wrestling team, had attacked a Negro boy, much smaller, in the cloakroom at recess. Miss Findlay threw him out of the class with both hands and a foot on his bottom. Miss Findlay made the white students sit by the Negroes and threatened to fail anyone who opened his mouth about it. When two white cheerleaders made whispered fun of a fat Negro girl, Miss Findlay put her arms around the sobbing child, and told the cheerleaders she was going to do everything she could to get them suspended for the rest of the year. Then she sent them back to Lytton High. They left smirking and switching their trim behinds, but there was unease in their blue eyes that had never been there before. Somehow nobody doubted that Miss Findlay could and would do what she said she would.

Students swarmed around Peyton when school was out. Was her cousin going to have Negro teachers over for dinner at Peyton's house? Was it true that she had made the white students use the Negro cloakrooms? Would the Negroes use the white ones when they came to Lytton High? Was she going to join St John's African Methodist Episcopal Church?

Nora laughed so hard when Peyton relayed these concerns that she choked on her cigarette and smoke exploded from her nostrils. 'Well, here's what you tell them,' she said. 'A: Maybe, if they ask me over to theirs first. B: If anybody wants to pee, they'll do it in the nearest bathroom, wherever that happens to be. C: I'll probably go to some services at St John's. I love the singing.'

'What did you do for your first class?'

'Well, after I got all the sniggering quieted down, I read to them from *To Kill a Mockingbird*. Then I picked out passages and asked them to read them aloud.'

'What parts?'

'The earliest parts, where Scout tells us about Maycomb, and about the people who lived there. I wanted them to see how close literature comes to the lives they know themselves, even though it happened in another time and place. And I think they got it, finally. Of course, none of them reads aloud very well, black or white, but towards the end nobody was embarrassed any more, and everyone was raising their hand to say how they thought Lytton was like Maycomb. They're very quick, if not articulate.'

'I wish I could take that class,' Peyton said. 'My English class is stupid. Mrs Manning just assigned us *Little Women*. I stopped reading that stuff when I was ten.'

'Well, I can't let you come to this one, but maybe we could sort of review what I've been doing in class every afternoon or so. You can read along with us. Or even better, you write down what you think about it and we'll go over it and compare it to what my high-schoolers said. I bet you'll be way ahead of them.'

'Maybe,' Peyton said. 'If you're still here next year, Nora, maybe I could take one of your classes. I'll almost be in high school then.'

'My Lord, so you will,' Nora said, looking at her and smiling. 'And you have a birthday this summer, too, don't you?'

'In June. Right after graduation.'

'Ah, graduation. Is there a commencement? When I started high school all you did was just show up.'

'Not really a commencement,' Peyton mumbled. She had been thinking with dread about that for some time. 'Just this thing in the school auditorium where the school choir sings and a preacher says something, and there are some speeches and stuff. It's not a big deal. I don't even think I'm going to go.'

Nora shot her a keen look. 'What sort of speeches?' she said. 'Who makes them?'

'Oh, you know. The ones who make good grades and stuff.'

'You'll be asked to make one.'

'No, I'm sure not. Besides, I'd hate it. I'd never in the world know what to say. I'd make such a fool of myself that I'd be the winner in the Losers Club for the rest of my life.'

Nora tapped her unlit cigarette thoughtfully on the table and studied her. 'The Losers Club. Is that the club you go to every afternoon? Why is it called that?'

'We tell each other what dumb things we've done that day, and the one who did the dumbest wins. It's usually Boot, because his foot makes him clumsy. He's always falling over things. It's really nothing. Just something we got in the habit of doing a long time ago. And it's not all stupid stuff. Ernie plays music for us and tells us about the theatre and literature and all.'

'Hmmm,' Nora said. 'Sounds like fun. Can I come sometime?'

'Well, it's in the bylaws that nobody but us can come. I asked Ernie and he got all cranky about it, but I'll ask him again. Boot would love it. He thinks your car is the greatest.'

'Never mind. I don't want to make Ernie uncomfortable. I'll meet Boot sometime here.'

Nora met Boot the next afternoon, when he came to the McKenzie house after the Losers Club. When she was much younger Peyton had played with him on those occasions, but at some point they had grown apart except for the Losers Club and, on those afternoons when he was visiting, Peyton was usually reading, and he pottered around the kitchen with his grandmother. It bothered neither Boot nor Peyton. At the Losers Club they were fully equal, and that was what counted.

Boot came in shortly after Peyton had got home, slamming the back door and shouting for his grandmother. Peyton heard, from the snug harbour of her bed, Chloe saying, 'Now, you just stay in this kitchen and be quiet. Peyton studying and Miss Nora coming in from the library any time now.'

'She comin' in that car?'

'Of course she is. You think she flying?'

'Maybe if I held the door for her she'd take me for a ride,' Boot said ingenuously. 'I could probably wash it sometime, too.'

Peyton heard the front door open and close, and heard Nora's voice: 'Is that the incomparable Meatloaf à la Chloe I smell?'

Peyton got up and went into the kitchen. No matter what her intentions about reading or listening to records, when Nora came into the house she was drawn out of her room like a moth to a leaping flame. Light and air and noise came in with Nora. The old house had not felt their like in Peyton's lifetime.

It must be what it was like when my mother was alive, she thought.

Nora dumped her armful of books onto the breakfast table and plopped down in her seat. 'Coffee before I die?' she said. 'And maybe some of that pecan pie from last night? Peyton, are you game for some? I swear I . . ." Her voice trailed off. Boot's grinning face had appeared round the door into the kitchen, 'Well, who have we here?'

'This is my grandbaby Boot,' Clothilde said. 'He promised not to bother anybody. Boot, this is Miss Nora. You know, I told you. She's staying with us for a while.'

'Hello, Boot,' Nora said, looking a him levelly. 'I've been hearing about you.'

He hung his head and dug at the linoleum with his toe, and then looked up at her and gave her the full wattage of his smile. 'I been hearin' about you, too,' he said. 'That your car out there?'

'It is,' Nora said, sipping her coffee and squinting at him through the steam.

'I heard you drove it all the way up here from Cuba.'

'Well, from Key West, Florida. That's about as far as you can go before you come to Cuba.'

'With the top down?'

'A lot of the time.'

'You get bugs squashed on you?'

Nora smiled then. 'Pounds and pounds of them.'

Boot's joyous, froggy laugh rang out. 'Ain't that somethin? Boy, I'd like to seen all them bugs . . .'

It was obviously time for Nora to say, 'I'll take you for a ride sometime,' but she did not. 'A few bugs go a long way,' she said.

There was a small silence, and then Boot said, 'You could drive that car to our club meeting sometime. It right up the street. And if it got bugs on it I could wash and wax it for you.'

'Well, I'll think about that,' Nora said, and she gathered up her books as if to leave. Peyton watched as Boot's heart leapt into his black eyes, and she knew she had just witnessed the thing they called love at first sight. Because Boot was staring at her cousin with such naked adoration, she said, 'Nora says she doesn't think she'll come to club meetings.'

'I bet you ain't never done nothin' stupid,' Boot said to Nora.

'Dumber than you can possibly imagine,' Nora said.

'Tell one!' Boot crowed with joy. This was too much for him, a copper-crowned madonna who drove around in a pink chariot and did dumb things.

'Maybe one day,' Nora said, and she went out of the room and up the stairs. Peyton stared after her. So did Boot and Chloe.

After Boot and Chloe had gone home, Nora came down to Peyton's room and settled onto the end of the narrow white bed as she sometimes did. 'What's happening, kiddo?' she said.

Peyton closed her book. 'Did Boot make you mad or something?' she said. 'He makes a lot of noise, I know, with that boot thing, but he's nice, and he can be real funny sometimes.'

Nora looked at her and then out the window into the back yard, where the first forsythia was beginning to spill like a fountain.

'I'm just not wild about children,' she said. 'There's no use pretending I am. I'll try to be nicer to Boot, though. I just hope he isn't underfoot all the time.'

Peyton saw a curtain fall behind Nora's green eyes. Something in her was closing like a door. There were secrets inside Nora, places she would allow no one to go. She realised that what she had been given of Nora was carefully edited, that an entire continent lay underneath.

As if possessed of some perverse incubus, Boot was indeed underfoot after that. His infatuation knew no bounds. Whenever Nora got out of her car in the afternoon, Boot would rush to hold the door for her, to carry her books and her parcels. Whenever, at a weekend, she set out on one of her slow cruises around town, she would see Boot in the rearview mirror, thumping after her like one of the Seven Dwarfs. Nora said nothing, but began to disappear into her room the minute she came home from school, and stopped coming down to breakfast, where, often, Boot would be lurking like a happy frog.

'Doesn't that child have anybody else to look after him?' she said once to Peyton, after Boot had offered once more to clean the Thunderbird.

'Well, we all sort of look after him,' Peyton said. 'And he's with me and Ernie almost every afternoon. He's never any trouble.'

'Maybe not to you,' Nora said under her breath, taking the stairs to her room two at a time.

Clothilde had, Peyton knew, recently forbidden Boot the house except in a real emergency. But Nora never mentioned him to Chloe, and Chloe did not speak of him, either.

Not until the day in March when Nora came home early from her tutoring session at the black high school and found Boot in her car, top down, engine running, radio booming out country music. Boot's eyes were squeezed shut, and his face was rapt with bliss. He did not see Nora until she jerked the car door open and clutched him by his collar and dragged him out of the car. Her face was blanched with fury, and her eyes were slitted. Peyton, watching through the screen door, gasped and went still. This was going to be bad.

Nora bent and looked into Boot's face, only inches from it. Her hands gripped his shoulders, and she shook him slightly. 'Don't you ever, *ever* touch my car again, you hear me? Don't come near it. Don't come near me. *Nobody* touches that car but me! Where did you get those keys?'

'They was laying on the kitchen table,' Boot whispered. He was trying to pull away from Nora's hands. She let him go abruptly, and he staggered a little, then took off round the house.

Nora stood with her head bent, her eyes closed. Then she turned towards the house. Peyton scuttled into her room. She did not want to talk about this. She did not want to see Nora's face like that. She did not want to see Boot's humiliation.

No one mentioned the incident at supper. Nora ate with relish and chatted of insignificant things, and Frazier took out the pipe he had resumed smoking and smiled at them both through sweet smoke. That night Peyton showed herself her movies. She wrote in her diary, *Even the air hurts*.

Nora finally went to Boot's house and apologised to him, largely, Peyton knew, because Chloe's face was so miserable. She didn't know what had come over her, she said, except that she was terribly tired and had not been sleeping well.

'Of course I'll take you for a ride in the car,' she said, and Chloe and Boot nodded in unison. But Boot did not come back to the house. Peyton saw him at the Losers Club, where he dutifully recited his litanies of abasement; she said nothing about Nora and the car because he did not know she knew about the incident. But he was somehow diminished, like a photograph left out in the sun, and though he could still make her and Ernie laugh, he did not often laugh with them. He was, somehow, a wise and wizened little man, not a child any more.

It seemed a long time before Chloe began to sing again in the kitchen.

6

On St Patrick's Day Nora took Peyton and Frazier into Atlanta for dinner.

'I think there's some sort of parade down Peachtree Street, too,' she said. 'We really ought to see it.'

'You want to take a Scotsman to a St Patrick's Day parade?' Frazier said. He was smiling, though.

'Why not? Loosen you up a little. We'll have you drinking green beer before you know it.'

'Faith and begorra,' he said. Peyton laughed happily. She could not remember her father ever making a real joke before.

It was a sweet, soft day, and they went in the Thunderbird, all three of them squeezed into the front seat. Nora laughed at the sight of Frazier folding his long body into the little pink car, sitting with his knees under his chin. Peyton, crammed between them, felt a swoop of joy that seemed to have its provenance in nothing at all but the rush of clean wind past her face.

They parked the Thunderbird in Davison's parking lot and walked up to Peachtree Street. Both sides of the street were crowded with people wearing all shades of green. Vendors were selling four-leaf clover pennants. Although Peyton could see no bars on the length of the street, there must have been ready sources for green beer because nearly everyone around them was carrying paper cups of it.

The parade itself was modest. The handsome, white-haired mayor came first, in a green Lincoln convertible, followed by sundry other dignitaries in convertibles. On a throne draped in green sat the queen of the parade, in a cloud of virulent green tulle and a headdress of woven shamrocks.

Behind the queen and her court came a band, and then a surging straggle of green-clad, beer-carrying people, waving banners and shillelaghs and singing. It was not a big parade, but it was a loud one, and when they got back into the Thunderbird to drive out along Peachtree Street to Buckhead, Peyton's ears still rang with it.

They had dinner in the same Italian restaurant where Peyton and Nora had eaten before. Nora and her father split a bottle of Chianti, and Peyton had a splash of it in a small glass. Her father ordered clam linguine for two, and Nora studied the menu and then said, 'Peyton, I think the scungili for you. It's light, and it has a nice lemony taste to it.'

'What is it?' Peyton said doubtfully.

'Fish cooked with some wine. Really special.'

'OK,' Peyton said. 'I'll try it.'

They talked in the flickering light of a candle, and the waiter hovered over Nora and brought another bottle of Chianti, 'on the house', he said. Nora smiled.

Their dinner came then. Peyton's plate was steaming, and a wonderful smell curled up from the browned medallions on it.

'Mmmm,' she said, taking a bite. The swirls of lemon butter and wine the fish was bathed in were exotic and rich. She finished most of it and mopped up the sauce with a piece of bread.

'That was good,' she said. 'What kind of fish did you say it was?'

Nora leaned back and lit a cigarette and smiled at her. 'Squid,' she said. 'Some people call it octopus.'

Peyton's stomach muscles contracted. And then they subsided. 'Not bad at all,' she said, thinking that the squid was going to earn her a place of honour in the pantheon of awfulness at the Losers Club. Let's see Ernie top that, she thought.

On the way home Nora put the top up on the Thunderbird. The inside of the car was small and dark and warm, and the radio played softly. Nora sang along with Dean Martin: 'Return to Me'. Her voice was soft and gritty. Wedged between them, Peyton closed her eyes and let the roaring of the road beneath them swell in her ears until she slipped off on its tide. Once she lifted her head and saw black, star-pricked sky and knew they were sailing through the fields near home. She heard laughter, and put her head back on her father's shoulder and slept again.

WHEN PEYTON CAME in from the Losers Club the next Monday, Nora told her the awful news. Her grandmother had suffered a stroke. It was severe, and Agnes McKenzie stayed in the hospital in Atlanta for weeks. She could not speak, and all efforts to make her accept therapy failed. When she was able to leave the hospital, Frazier found a nearby nursing home for her. It was clean, cheerful, and well staffed, and it cost the very earth. Agnes seemed, if not happy, then at least content there.

Peyton visited often at first, but she could not be sure that her grandmother even knew her. Nora visited once, with Frazier, and her grandmother became violent, trying to rip out her tubes—trying, it seemed, to get at Nora. That night she had another small stroke, and after that she was gone from them, only her slight body remaining.

Peyton did not visit any more after that. Only Frazier went, night after night, to hold his mother's hands. When he came home from these visits he usually spent an hour or so in his office before he came in to watch television with them.

After her last visit to her grandmother, Peyton wrote in her diary, *Why do people have to be wrecked like that? Who will there be in my life like her now?*

In her heart she knew the answer to that, but she could not bear the weight of it, and buried it deep.

ALL THROUGH the early days of that spring, Nora incised herself deeply and vividly into the small life of Lytton. It was as if, content that she had safe harbour in the house on Green Street, she felt emboldened to flash out into the town and the school like a comet, trailing delight and outrage in equal parts in her wake.

Late afternoons became Nora and Peyton's special time together. Much of it was spent up in Nora's room, Nora with her long length curled on her bed, smoking, Peyton in the red canvas butterfly chair her cousin had brought with her, a hectic anomaly in that dim room of polished mahogany and white chenille. Trailways would desert Peyton temporarily to curl into the curve of Nora's waist or legs, and knead with his sharp claws and purr his rusty, room-shaking purr.

They talked endlessly, but almost never about themselves. It was too soon for that. They talked about books, about music, about movies. Or rather, Nora talked. Peyton had no sense of being instructed, but she knew in some way that Nora was tutoring her. She began, once in a while, to venture an opinion about whatever it was they were talking about.

'Why do you listen to me?' she asked Nora once. 'I don't know anything about anything yet.'

'You will.' Nora smiled.

Sometimes, in the warming nights, they did things: they went, the three of them, to a movie in Atlanta occasionally, or a symphony at the Municipal Auditorium, and once to *Our Town*, a play put on by an Atlanta company. Nora said it was oversentimental claptrap and overdone, but she wept along with Peyton when the dead of Grover's Corners reached out, in vain, to the living. They went to a couple of baseball games, and once to a square dance at the Lytton Veterans hut. Frazier laughingly refused to dance, and Peyton would not have if someone had held a gun to her head, but Nora danced every set with every man who asked her.

Once, in the middle of a tender night heavy with the smell of wisteria, Nora woke Peyton and they took the Thunderbird, top down, out into the country to a small lake that fed into the Lytton reservoir, where they slipped naked into the blood-warm water and swam under the moon.

But mostly Nora seemed to want simply to be in the house on Green Street. Sometimes, after dinner, instead of watching television, she would read to them out of whatever esoteric book she was reading, and once in a while she made martinis before dinner and she and Frazier had one. Peyton ate the olives.

Peyton knew via the grammar school jungle drums that almost none of the female teachers at Lytton High liked Nora, and that most of the male ones did, and that almost every unmarried male teacher had asked her out. But she never talked about it, and she never went out on a date.

'You should get out some,' Frazier said. 'It's just not right for you to sit in this old house all the time when you should be out meeting people your own age.'

'Maybe later,' Nora said. 'Right now I'd rather just be here with you all. You have no idea how tired of flitting around I am.'

'Didn't you date in Florida and Cuba?' Peyton asked her in one of their late-night talk sessions on Nora's bed, where Nora sometimes let her have a drag of a Salem. In her head, Peyton had invented a lavish, exotic life for Nora back in those fabled cities she had left. Men were a large part of it—handsome, mysterious men unlike any she knew in Lytton. There must have been men.

'She's had hundreds of affairs,' Peyton told the Losers Club. 'She had lovers in every city, but eventually she got bored with them and left. I think she still gets letters from some of them.'

'Tell about that,' Boot said, enchanted.

Ernie sniffed. 'If she had all those lovers it seems to me one of them might have finally married her,' he said.

'She doesn't want to be tied down,' Peyton said. 'She told me that.'

Nora had done no such thing, but Peyton thought it was true.

Nora would not talk about Cuba or Miami or Key West, at least not about the men she had known there, except to say that of course she had had dates, but for now no one was as interesting as the people in this funny old house. Peyton could not imagine why anyone would think her or her father interesting, but she was warmed as she could not remember having been in her life. She mattered, at last, to someone who did not have to love her.

'You know, Chloe,' Nora said one morning, 'I promised you and Doreen that I'd tutor her in the afternoons so she can get her high school equivalency certificate. Would you tell her that now would be a good time for us to start?'

Chloe looked down at the sinkful of tomato peels. 'Doreen ain't around afternoons no more,' she said. 'She got a job up in Hapeville at the McDonald's. They likes her a lot. Look like she be able to be an assistant manager in a year or two.'

Nora stared at her. 'Chloe, she doesn't need to sling hamburgers all her life!' she said. 'No telling where she might go if she gets that certificate. Why on earth did she leave Mrs McKenzie's? I know she's awful, but at least Doreen had enough free time to study.'

Chloe was silent, and then she said, 'She ain't leave. Miss Augusta fired her. Didn't even give her no notice.'

'Why?' Nora cried. 'Who on earth wouldn't want Doreen working for them?'

'She come home from church early and found Doreen sittin' in the bathtub,' Chloe said without looking at Peyton or Nora. 'She like to bust a gut. She tell Doreen to put on her clothes and get out and not come back. She didn't even give her time to dry off. Doreen come home with her clothes all wet.'

'Oh, *Chloe*,' Nora said, stricken.

'Thing is, Doreen ain't never had no bathtub,' Chloe said. 'We always wash in washtubs. I guess she just wanted to see how it felt to sit down in that hot water. It ain't like Miss Augusta was going to catch anything from her. Doreen is a clean girl. You can get mighty clean in a washtub.'

Peyton watched Nora's face in silence. It was blanched white and there was a spot of red high on each cheekbone. She went out of the room silently and did not open her bedroom door that afternoon to Peyton and Trailways.

That evening Peyton heard her father's car door slam out front, and at almost the same instant heard Nora's running steps on the stairs. She went to her own bedroom door and opened it an inch or so, but she did not go out into the living room.

'Do you know what that woman has done?' she heard Nora shout.

'What woman?' her father said. His voice was alarmed.

'Your sister-in-law! The famous Augusta McKenzie of Lytton, Georgia, social and moral arbiter to a generation, font of compassion for the frail and lowly—'

'Sit down,' Frazier McKenzie said. 'Tell me.'

'I hate her, Frazier,' Peyton heard her cousin say. Her voice was trembling. 'She is the worst, most evil woman I have ever known.'

'Nora, what has she *done*?'

'She fired Doreen because she found her in her bathtub,' Nora said. 'She thought Doreen had contaminated it.'

And she burst into tears.

There was a brief silence, and then Nora continued, her voice strangled with sobs. 'You know, we said I was going to tutor Doreen so she could get her reading up to par and take the high school equivalency test. You were there that day at lunch. So this morning I told Chloe I'd like to start and she told me that Doreen had been fired and was working at the McDonald's up in Hapeville. Frazier, what future can she possibly have now? Oh, I *hate* Augusta . . .'

There was a silence in which only Nora's muffled sobs resounded. Peyton opened her door a few more inches and peered out. Nora sat on the sofa with her face in her hands. Her father, looking drawn and weary, sat beside her, patting her awkwardly on the back.

'Nora,' he said presently. 'You need to understand about Augusta. I don't mean to excuse her; what she did was an ugly thing. A lot of what she does is downright unacceptable. But we do accept it, our family, because we know what she came out of, we know how hard she's worked building a life for herself.'

'What life?' Nora cried. 'It's certainly no life for Charlie! It's certainly no life for Peyton. What life are you talking about?'

'She was born in a mill-village shack,' Peyton's father said slowly. 'It was worse, in a way, than most of our Negro neighbourhoods because the folks who live there have strong family ties and often white families who care for them. But they didn't have that in Augusta's little settlement. Everybody was too intent on digging his own way out to put out a hand to a neighbour. A lot of them just gave up. Augusta's parents were like that. When Charlie met her, her father was dying of white lung and still smoking like a chimney, lying on an old sofa they had dragged out onto the front porch. Her mother was drunk most of the time. There was an older brother who had long since left and was in jail in the North somewhere. And there was a younger sister, about eleven, who stayed out of school and did whatever she pleased. Augusta was the pretty one, and the smart one, and she really is both of those things. She worked at the perfume counter at Rich's in Atlanta, and she taught herself how to act like a lady and dress like one on the measly little salary she made. It can't have been much, and she had to pay a lot of the family's rent and grocery bills every month, and keep her little sister in clothes, because both the parents were on disability.

'So one day Charlie went into Rich's to buy Mother some perfume for Christmas, and he took one look at her, and that was that. She sold herself right along with the perfume. They were married not three months later. I guess she thought she was marrying way up with Charlie, but I think if she'd known him a little longer she'd have realised that what she saw in Charlie was what she was going to get. I love Charlie; he's my brother and he's a sweet man. But he's no Prince Charming, no rescuer of maidens. Augusta never got over that. She'd seen herself as totally safe and secure, the most socially sought-after woman in this part of the county, the absolute oracle of manners and propriety and elegance. But I guess she's known for a long time now that she's only as safe as Charlie's last pay cheque, and the only people she can lord it over are her servants and sometimes my daughter. She's forgotten that Charlie gave her two things she'd never have had without him: a ticket out of the mill village and his love. He really loves her. Always has. Don't think he doesn't know how disappointed in him she is. It's made her mean. We all know that. Most of us have learned just to overlook the silliest of her pranks and dodge the really hurtful ones. I sometimes think she really does care about Peyton and me, but I can't think why . . .'

'Oh, Frazier!' Nora said. 'If you can't think why, then you're more oblivious than I thought. It's obvious. She's got an awful crush on you, and she's trying to get at you through Peyton.'

'Oh, I don't think so,' Frazier said doubtfully. 'But you're right about this thing with Doreen. We can't let that go. I'll talk to her about it. Maybe she'll take Doreen back. If she won't, maybe I can find her something closer to home that will give her time to study, and maybe we can help her out a little financially . . .'

'Frazier McKenzie,' Nora said, tears in her voice again. 'You are maybe the best man I've ever known.'

'Then God help you,' Frazier said. Peyton could hear the smile in his voice. 'Will you at least try to think a little better of Augusta now?'

'No,' Nora said. 'She's a bitch and I hate her. But I'll lay off her unless she does something else this bad, which she'll probably manage to do tomorrow.'

Peyton went into the bathroom and washed her face for dinner. She felt lighter than air. She knew that whatever bonds kept her tethered to earth, they were never again going to be of Aunt Augusta's making.

WHEN SHE NEXT WENT to the Losers Club, Peyton realised she had not been going so often and felt guilty and somehow resentful. She was tired of having to make excuses to Ernie. She was aware, as she knew he was, that she was lying regularly to the club when she said that Nora was tutoring her after school. It seemed that he reported on Nora's public antics with far more venom and less delectation than usual, and it occurred to her that he was punishing her with the stories.

'Have you met Mr Lloyd Huey, who lives next door to your Aunt Augusta and Uncle Charles?' he asked, and when Peyton said that of course she knew him, Ernie continued.

'Well, then, you know he owns the sawmill and has a bunch of Negroes working for him. He also has an enormous fallout shelter in his backyard. Well, somehow Nora got the notion that he was mistreating his help, and she told him in the drugstore that if he didn't shape up she was going to tell everybody in town that he had asked her down to see the famous shelter and then tried to seduce her. It's the kind of talk that could ruin a man in a little town like this.'

'How could it ruin Mr Huey?' Peyton said. 'He's got five children and only one leg and he's in a wheelchair all the time.'

'Well, I guess Nora thinks that any man with breath in his body would try to seduce her, and she may be right. God knows, enough of them have.'

'I'm going home,' Peyton said, sudden anger shaking her. 'You've turned the club into a witch-hunt against Nora. That's not fair, and it's not fun any longer.'

'The truth is often not much fun,' Ernie said unctuously.

Peyton slammed out of the shed and stamped home, a feeling of heaviness and loss hanging over her.

When she got home her father and her Uncle Charlie were coming out of the living room. Charles McKenzie looked miserable. Behind him, her father's face was set. Peyton murmured hello to both of them and slid into her room like a salamander going to earth. On this day of strangeness, nothing good was going to come of this visit. She knew it.

She peered through the almost-closed door of her room at her father, thinking that she was getting quite good at spying on people and not caring. He sat down in his accustomed chair and stared straight ahead. He did not open his newspaper or turn on the television set. This was as strange to Peyton as the fact of his being in the living room at all before dinner, when daylight still filtered through the drawn blinds. This room was his nighttime place.

She was about to close her door and curl up with Trailways when she heard Nora's light step on the porch, and the screened door creaking open and shut again.

'Well, what on earth are you doing in here in the daylight?' Peyton heard her say. There was a silence, and then Frazier said, 'Come in and sit down, Nora. We need to talk a little.'

Peyton froze at her spying post. Whatever great trouble this meeting portended, she needed to know about it. At the last minute she moved back from her door so that she could hear but not see. Somehow she could handle an assault on one sense but not on two.

'Charles was here,' her father said. 'He was pretty upset. I've never known him to tell tales on anyone, but he felt like he had to tell me about this. Lloyd Huey came over to see him this afternoon and told him what you said to him in the drugstore. Lloyd was mad and he was hurt. He thought Charlie would be the right one to tell me about it, and then he wanted me to speak to you.'

There was a silence. Peyton could imagine them sitting there, her father leaning forward with his hands clasped and resting on his knees, Nora slumping in the other chair and lighting a cigarette.

'This is pretty serious, Nora,' her father said. 'I don't think we can let it go as one more of your . . . escapades. The others have been on the side of the angels, even if they stirred up hornets' nests all over town. A certain amount of that is good for Lytton. But this has really hurt Lloyd. Charlie said he had tears in his eyes when he came over.'

There was another silence. Then her father went on: 'Nora, Lloyd is insensitive, to say the least. And I think he probably is tough on his help over at the mill. But I seriously doubt he mistreats Negroes. He may yell at them, but he yells at everybody. We let it go because it's a tough life he's living and because his mill has provided jobs for a whole lot of people, Negroes mostly. That kind of talk can hurt him in the town. Whether or not people believe it in the beginning, they'll talk.'

'Oh, Frazier,' Nora whispered. 'I really did hear that he abused his Negro workers physically, and withheld their pay when they displeased him. You know we can't let that go by—'

'What is this "we", Nora?' Frazier McKenzie said, and Peyton heard the ice in his voice.

'I can't imagine you would sanction that sort of thing,' Nora said. Her voice seemed to be losing force with every word.

'I wouldn't sanction that sort of thing if it were true, but it can't possibly be,' her father said. 'I've known Lloyd since we were kids. If he was seriously abusing his Negro help it would have got out way before now. The fact is you've jumped to a bad conclusion, and you've taken way too much on yourself. You cannot just come into this town and set yourself up as an avenging angel. It hurts people, and it will hurt you.'

'So what do you want me to do?' Nora whispered.

'I want you to go over and apologise to Lloyd,' her father said, 'and I want you just to stop with the . . . eccentricities. Just give it all a rest for a while. Even if I agree with you, and sometimes I do, I just don't have the energy to go on cleaning up after you.'

Nora gave a gasp of hurt and leapt out of her chair and ran up the stairs. Peyton heard the door to her room close. But before that, she heard the ragged catch of a sob. Peyton crawled under her afghan with Trailways and lay there until supper time. Nora did not come down, and her father did not speak. They ate in silence, and he went out to his office over the garage, and Peyton went back to bed and cried. She could not bear the trouble humming in the air.

For a couple of days Nora avoided all of them, eating her meals standing up at the refrigerator at odd times of the day and night, leaving for school early in the morning, and staying away somewhere until very late. The Thunderbird was not often at the kerb. Peyton's father ate his meals silently, the newspaper unfolded before him, and went early to his office and stayed late. Chloe did not sing, or linger to talk, or make special desserts. Peyton went back to showing herself her movies at night.

On the fourth day she heard her cousin's steps clicking rapidly up the path and into and through the house to the back door. She pulled aside her curtain and looked. Nora, windblown and scarlet-cheeked, ran up the steps to her father's office and rapped smartly on the door. When she saw the door open, Peyton dropped the curtain and burrowed under her afghan again. This was nothing to spy on.

Nora and her father did not come down for a long time. Peyton was foraging hungrily in the kitchen when they did, lifting the lids of the pots Clothilde had left on the stove, rummaging in the pantry for biscuits. Nora was red-nosed and pouchy about the eyes, but the vivid life was back. Coming into the kitchen, she crackled with it. Peyton looked sideways at her father. His face was still grave and level, but the ice had gone from his eyes, and the crinkles at their corners looked freshly incised, as if he had been smiling. Peyton's heart, for days bound and shut down in her chest, now soared. It was going to be all right . . .

'What are you doing in here munching like a goat?' Nora said teasingly. The rich music was back in her voice. 'The least you could have done was heat up supper and set the table.'

'I don't know where all that stuff is,' Peyton said, pretending it was ordinary talk on an ordinary day. 'I don't know how to work the stove.'

'That's absurd,' Nora said. 'I could cook when I was ten years old. Knowing how to cook well is a very sexy thing. This coming Saturday you're going to start learning.'

She set the green beans and new potatoes to warm and wrapped the chicken in foil and put it in the oven. Then she made martinis. Peyton heard them laughing desultorily at something when she went in to change for dinner. She snatched up Trailways and danced him around her room and squeezed him until he growled. Then she went into the living room to warm herself and eat olives. She would never know what had passed between Nora and her father in his office that evening, nor whether Nora finally apologised to Mr Lloyd Huey. Whatever it was, it sufficed.

Two nights later her father came home early from the courthouse in Atlanta. She heard Nora's steps come down to meet him, and something low being said between them. Her father laughed, and then Nora called, 'Peyton! Get out here! Your days of innocence are over!'

Peyton went cautiously into the living room. Nora had been almost manic since the trouble had passed; a shimmering like heat lightning was on her. It made Peyton want to hug her and pull away from her at the same time. Nora could burn you as easily as she could warm you, she thought.

Nora had brought her portable gramophone downstairs. She stood in the middle of the room, grinning. She wore blue jeans and a T-shirt, and her freshly washed hair almost gave off sparks. Peyton's father sat in his chair, smiling faintly at her.

'We are about to learn the twist,' Nora said. 'There is no hanging back and no salvation from it. By supper time I want to see those hips wiggling like there's no tomorrow.'

She put a record on the machine and started it.

'Come on, baby,' Chubby Checker growled. 'Let's do the twist . . .'

In the middle of the room, Nora planted her feet and threw back her head and held her hands out as if in a gesture of submission or supplication. Her hips began to gyrate in a circle but her feet remained planted. She seemed to swell with the music, until her whole body was bobbing on the surface of the insistent beat.

Peyton felt her face burn but something in her own hips and pelvis responded to the tug of the music. She smiled.

'Come on,' Nora said. 'Both of you, get out here. No, Frazier, you aren't going to chicken out of this. I've always thought you could dance like a demon if you wanted to. Keep your feet still—that's right—and just move your hips in a kind of circle, in time to the music. Come on, Peyton.'

The music and motion took Peyton and flung her far away, and when she came back she was doing the twist as if she had known how all her life. Her hips seemed to move themselves, knowing this old rhythm. She laughed aloud and looked over at her father. He danced fluidly opposite Nora. His dark hair hung over his eyes, and he was laughing.

The record ended and Nora put it on again. By the time it had played itself out two or three times they were flushed and sweating and moving as loosely as if their joints had been oiled. They had just sagged, laughing, into chairs and the sofa when Chloe came into the room. She stood in the doorway, not speaking. Her face was ashen under its deep ochre. There were tears in her eyes.

'I don't reckon y'all heard the phone,' she said. 'Miss Agnes done passed.'

Late that night Peyton heard her father come into the living room. He had been to the nursing home and then to the funeral home, making arrangements. His step was slow and heavy. Peyton did not get out of bed. The abrupt draining of the exhilaration of the afternoon and the cold nothingness of her grandmother's death had tired her beyond rising. She turned into her pillow and hugged Trailways and closed her eyes once more. Even when she heard Nora come rapidly down the stairs from her room, she did not get up. Let them deal with it, this heavy blankness that was death.

Then she heard the sound of sobbing, dry and rough, as though the weeper did not know how to do it, and she got up and went to her door.

Her father sat slumped on the sofa. Nora knelt beside him, her arms around him, his face pressed into her shoulder. She was rocking him slightly, back and forth, and her face was pressed into his dark hair.

Peyton averted her eyes and, trembling all over, got the long-unworn amulet her grandmother had given her from her jewellery box, dropped it over her head and looked down. I'm getting breasts, she thought, and my grandmother is dead and my father is crying.

She slept heavily and long and got up aching as if she had been beaten. Neither her father nor Nora was about, and Chloe was silent in the kitchen as she put toast and eggs on the table.

'They gone to pick out a casket,' she said. 'You go on to school, now. There ain't nothing you can do till later.'

After school Peyton went as straight and swiftly as an arrow to the Losers Club. She longed with every atom of her being to be in a place where no strangeness was. When she got there, the door was padlocked. She went round to the window and stood on a cement block that lay under it. The chairs were gone, and the space heater, and the shelf that had held Ernie's library. Only the potbellied stove remained, black and empty.

Peyton walked home sobbing aloud.

Why is it, she wrote in her diary that night, *that if you have one thing you can't have another?*

7

After that, Peyton became obsessed with her Cousin Nora. She dogged her steps in the daytime, leaned close to her when they watched television at night. Everything Nora did and said and thought seemed, in these days, to be touched with mystery and glamour, and Peyton could not get enough of them.

One Saturday in May Nora went in the afternoon to tutor a Negro child in English.

'*Huckleberry Finn,*' she said, getting into the Thunderbird. 'He's having a hard time with Jim. I think it's the first time he's ever really thought about what slavery meant.'

She drove away and Peyton went back into the house, scuffling her sandals in the gravel of the driveway. Her father was in his office, and Chloe had gone home. Peyton went in search of Trailways. She knew he would be on Nora's bed, lying on his back with his big paws folded on his mottled belly.

Peyton went up the stairs into Nora's room, knowing precisely what she was going to do and on fire with it. She closed the door behind her and opened the door to Nora's closet and looked on the top shelf. The ebony box was there, behind a warped tennis racket. It seemed to shine like a beacon in the gloom of the closet. Trembling, she lifted the box from the shelf and carried it over to Nora's bed. Part of the tremor was the fear of being caught and horror at what she was doing. Part of it was an anticipation so keen that it took her breath.

Peyton set the chest down on the bed. She took a deep breath and felt for the latch on the box. It was unlocked and opened easily.

She closed her eyes and breathed, 'I'm sorry for doing this, God,' and looked into the box for the core of her Cousin Nora.

Papers. Nothing but papers and envelopes. The papers seemed to be ordinary documents: birth certificate, passport, copy of a driver's licence, the sale papers and title to the Thunderbird. Some of the envelopes held letters, but they were disappointing: chatty notes from unknown women friends, a couple that might have been from tepid boyfriends. Nothing else. No photographs, no treasured bits of jewellery. Peyton leaned back, disappointment flooding her. Where was Nora in all this? Where was the source of the mystery that was so close it was almost palpable?

She started to close the box, and then she saw that the old velvet lining was slit at its top, some of the fabric rotting away. Her fingers felt the bulk of papers. Without hesitating she reached in and pulled out a thick manila envelope.

Photographs. Here she was, then. Here was Nora. Peyton's heart thudded high in her throat. She shuffled them slowly. The first few were landscapes, undistinguished and rather flat, with a low jumble of industrial buildings in the background. A shot of an ocean, clouds massing over its horizon, scabby palm trees in the foreground. Then a square in a town, with children darting about in the dirt street, laughing. Flowers hanging low from trees and bursting from pots and window boxes. Even in its obvious poverty and banality, the square had a holiday air.

The next photograph was the same view, but in its midst, beside a dry fountain in the middle of the square, stood the virulently pink Thunderbird. Peyton's breath caught.

She lifted the photograph and took out the others. They were of people, people and Nora. Nora, her red hair molten in the sun, black sunglasses on her nose, laughing with her arms round a man and an old woman. A small group of people stood behind them. Nora wore short shorts and a peasant blouse. The men wore trousers and bright flowered shirts, the women cotton skirts and tops like Nora's. The old woman held a child in her arms, and there were other children at the feet of the adults. All the people except Nora were black. Against them, Nora burned like a pale flame.

Peyton thought that this must be the family Nora had lived with in Cuba. They were handsome people, but their blackness was so absolute that it was startling. Peyton had always thought Cubans were white with black hair and moustaches.

She picked up another photograph and saw the Thunderbird again, this time silhouetted against a beach. Here were the white sand and blue skies and turquoise water she had imagined; here was the paradisiacal backdrop she had built in her mind for Nora. There was no one in the Thunderbird. A faded inscription on the back of the photograph read *The famous Thunderbird, 1955.*

Beneath it was another photograph of the Thunderbird, only this time Nora was sitting in it, smiling at the camera, holding a small child in her arms, her cheek pressed into his hair. The child was reaching out to touch the glittering mirror on the driver's side. The sun was high; Nora's hair shone a pure, burnished red.

So did the child's.

Peyton's breath stopped in her throat. Slowly she turned the photo over. *Madonna and child* was written in Nora's slashing backhand. *Me and the baby, summer 1957.*

Whose child it was had not been written there. There was no need. Peyton knew. She closed the box and sat down on the edge of Nora's bed, trembling all over, her mind working feverishly to assimilate the photograph.

Nora had a child, a midnight-dark Cuban child with impossible red hair. He was perhaps a year old in the photograph. Nora obviously loved him. He was just as obviously gone from her life now.

Peyton sat there for a long time. She looked at the photo, but she heard and saw nothing. Then she did: the door opening, and Nora's footsteps coming into the room. Peyton did not lift her head. She wished that she could simply die, sitting there.

She felt rather than saw Nora sit down on the edge of the bed beside her. Nora did not speak, but she reached out and took the photograph from Peyton's fingers.

'I'm sorry,' Peyton whispered. Her voice was strangled.

Nora said, 'Don't be. I would have told you sometime. I wasn't quite ready to do it now, but now's as good a time as any. The baby is my son. His name is Roberto. He adored that car. I could always stop him from crying just by putting him in it.'

'Is that why it made you so mad when Boot got in your car?'

'I wasn't mad. But yes, that's what . . . got to me. For a minute it was like seeing Roberto when he would be eight or nine.'

'Like Boot?'

'Yes. Roberto is very black, as I'm sure you've noticed.'

'Where is he?' Peyton said, and then wished she had bitten out her tongue. It was obvious something had happened with the baby or else he would be with Nora.

'He's in Cuba, with his grandmother,' Nora said. 'If you've seen the other photographs, she's the old woman. She loves him very much. When I was about to bring him back to Miami with me, she hid him away somewhere. I get letters from her sometimes, telling me about him. I know that he's safe and happy. I probably never will know where he is, unless he finds me when he's older.'

'Weren't you scared for him?' Peyton said. 'Couldn't you have called the police or something?'

Nora laughed. There was little of amusement in it. 'The police probably helped hide him. The law in Cuba is very flexible. It expands to fit whatever it needs to. No, I wasn't scared for him, and I'm still not. Cubans adore children; they're all that most of them have. The whole village will be Roberto's family. They'd never have let me take him away. Oh, they wouldn't have harmed me; the family I lived with loved me. But I was essentially an outsider, and Roberto wasn't. He's the jewel of the family. He'll have a better life in Cuba, even in that poor little village, than I could have given him here in the South. His colour would have made him a pariah, no matter how hard I tried to protect him. I couldn't have borne that.'

'Don't you miss him?'

'Like my arms and legs,' Nora said. 'Like my heart.'

Peyton felt a pang that was different from the shock of surprise and the surge of pity for Nora. It was jealousy.

'Will you go back there?' she said finally.

'No,' Nora said.

The silence spun out. Hesitantly, Peyton said, 'Does your husband help take care of him?'

Nora turned her head and smiled down at her.

'He's not my husband,' she said. 'He's a beautiful man, a sweet man. He adored me, and the baby is simply his heart. But when I . . . knew I had to come back, he wouldn't come with me. He was very angry. He had assumed I would stay in Cuba with them always. He helped his mother hide Roberto, and then he went into the mountains with Castro. He doesn't write. I presume he comes down to see Roberto occasionally, but I don't know where he is.'

'Maybe he'll bring Roberto here one day,' Peyton said.

'He'll never leave Cuba,' Nora said.

They were quiet again. 'It's awful,' Peyton said at last.

'Yes, it is,' Nora said. 'It wasn't smart of me. But I don't regret it. Raoul was the lover of a lifetime, and Roberto is in the world now. I'll always have those two things.'

Another silence, and then Nora said, 'You mustn't tell anyone, Peyton. Not anyone, not even your father. I'll have to decide when I'll do that, or even *if* I will. If anyone else knew I'd have to leave.'

'Daddy wouldn't care!'

'Maybe not, but there's no way it wouldn't get out eventually. Augusta would ruin both of you in a minute, just to get at me. I couldn't stay here. The rural South simply will not have it.'

Peyton's heart hurt. 'I promise,' she said. 'I'll never, ever tell anybody. It'll always be just our secret.'

After a time Nora stretched out on the bed and gathered Trailways to her and smiled up at Peyton. Her eyes were wet. Peyton was so giddy with shock and pride that Nora had confided in her that she could not speak.

'It seems to me that you know my secret now,' Nora said. 'But I don't know any of yours.'

'I don't have any secrets. I've never done anything,' Peyton said, feeling inadequate. Never, not even at the Losers Club, had she felt so utterly bereft.

'The best secrets can be the ones that you make with your mind,' Nora said. 'Didn't you ever have a secret dream? Didn't you want to be a ballet dancer or a spy or something when you got older? Didn't you ever have a great love affair in your mind?'

'No,' said Peyton, wincing.

'Oh, Peyton. The day that you will isn't far away at all. Don't be afraid of it. It won't happen until you're ready. And it's just the greatest thing, to be crazy in love with somebody. You wouldn't want to miss that.'

'I'll never get married,' Peyton said.

'I'm not talking about marriage,' Nora said, smiling.

Peyton blushed. 'I do have a secret,' she said suddenly. 'I have a huge one. I don't know how I could have forgotten.'

'And it is?' Nora said.

'I killed my mother.'

And this time, unlike the time at the Losers Club, Peyton did not feel dizzy with the enormity of it, only as if she had handed off something heavy to Nora.

Nora stared at her. 'What are you talking about?'

'Well . . . she bled to death after she had me. Didn't you know that?' Peyton said.

'Who told you that?' Nora's face was whitening as she spoke.

'Aunt Augusta. I must have been seven or eight.'

'And she told you you killed your mother?'

'Oh, no. Nobody had to tell me that. I mean, if I came and then she bled to death, what else could it be?'

'Peyton, did you ever talk to your father about this?'

Peyton looked down. 'No. We never talked about her. Not much, anyway. Every now and then I'd ask Chloe about her, and I have some old home movies with her in them, but I never asked Daddy about her.'

'Why in hell not?' Nora cried. Peyton fllnched. There was hot anger in Nora's voice.

'I thought he was grieving for her too much,' Peyton said. 'And then Buddy . . . I thought it would be just too awful to remind him. I guess I thought it was enough that he thought about it every time he looked at me.' She felt the old salt in her throat.

Nora sat up and reached over, took Peyton's face in her hands and held firm. 'Now listen,' she said. 'I have something to tell you, and I want you to be looking at me when I do. It's about your mother, and you have to know it now. It's way past time.'

Peyton looked steadily at her cousin, unable to move her head.

Nora pursed her lips and blew air through them. Then she said, 'Peyton, you did not kill your mother. Your mother was just fine when you were born. She was bleeding a little, but a lot of women do. The doctor propped her legs up on a pillow and told her not to get up until the next morning, and he gave her a shot of something. She was asleep when he left. Your father and your aunt were taking care of you. Your father was ecstatic.'

Peyton's heart filled. He had held her, then, had looked down at her, had rejoiced that she was in the world.

'What happened, then, if she was all right?' she said in a low, fearful voice.

'What happened was that she got out of bed that afternoon and slipped out and drove to the country club and shacked up with the tennis pro,' Nora said calmly. 'She'd been doing it for months. She must have been out of her mind. She came home and bled to death in the bathroom. The tennis pro was gone the next morning.'

A great whispering whiteness, like snow, filled Peyton's heart and mind. She looked into it as if she were looking at a blizzard through a windowpane. 'How do you know?'

'My mother told me. I don't know how she knew, but someone in the family obviously got wind of it, and told her. She told me not long before she died. I think now she told me out of spite. She and Lila Lee were always enemies.'

'Did . . . does my father know?' Peyton whispered.

'Yes,' Nora said.

'But he couldn't have told me,' Peyton said. 'He loved her so much. And he must have thought it would have hurt me awfully if he told me. . . . It was a kind thing, really.'

'I don't happen to think it's too terribly kind to let your child think that she killed her mother,' Nora said in a constricted voice.

'He didn't know I thought that. I've never told anybody that, except the Losers Club and now you.'

'Well, anybody with eyes could have seen that something's been bothering you all these years. He *should* have found out what it was, and the hell with his tender sensibilities.'

'Please don't be mad at him,' Peyton said, beginning to cry. She felt nothing about her mother, only the terrible possibility of the loss of Nora.

Nora got up. 'I'm going out to have a talk with your father,' she said, cheeks flaming. 'I want you to stay here until I come back and call you. I do not want you listening at the door this time. Oh, yeah, I know you do. I don't usually care, but I care about this. Hear what I'm saying, Peyton: if you eavesdrop on us I will know it and I will leave here this afternoon. Do you understand me?'

'Yes,' Peyton said through thick, stinging tears.

Nora had reached the door when Peyton cried, 'Wait! Could he be my . . . could I be . . . ?'

'God, no,' Nora said. 'You're every inch a McKenzie. He was a Neanderthal. His eyebrows met over his nose.'

She flung herself out of the room and slammed the door. Peyton pulled Trailways to her and curled into a ball around him. She stayed there until the cat fell asleep and the light outside the window went from yellow to blue, until she finally dozed.

She did not wake until Nora opened the door and put her head into the room. 'Your father and I are going to get a hamburger,' she said. Her voice was level, even light. There were silver tracks on her cheeks, though. She had been crying. 'There's cold roast beef in the fridge. Or we'll bring you a hamburger. But this time you can't come with us.'

'A hamburger would be nice,' Peyton said meekly.

But she had fallen asleep again long before they returned.

Peyton slept until morning, and when she woke she felt so much lighter that she thought she might float. Her mother was not, after all, a saint, and she herself was not a killer.

Presently Nora tapped on her door and then came in. She was dressed in her church 'lady' outfit, a soft yellow linen suit with a short jacket. The yellow linen cast a glow upon her neck and washed her tawny face faintly, as if she had held a bouquet of buttercups under her chin. Peyton thought she looked wonderful.

'You OK, kiddo?' Nora said, sitting down on the edge of Peyton's bed. 'You had a big day yesterday.'

'I feel funny,' Peyton said dreamily. 'Kind of floaty. Nothing seems very real. It almost feels like I'm in a place I don't know.'

'Well, in a way you are,' Nora said. 'Everything that shaped the world for you all your life changed yesterday. You want to talk about any of it?'

Peyton considered. 'I guess there's a lot I want to know about my mother,' she said. 'Will I ever know what she really was?'

'If you want to—as much as anyone knows anyone else. I'll tell you everything I know whenever you ask. Your father will talk to you about her, too. He hasn't before now because he thought it would be too hard for you. But he's promised that he will.'

'Did you all have a fight about this?'

'Mmm-hmm. A monstrous one. We were furious with each other. We yelled and screamed. Finally it occurred to both of us that this was not about us, it was about you, and then everything seemed just to fall into place. He knows he should have been closer to you all these years. He wanted to spare you any pain, and so he just didn't talk to you about anything. That's going to change, though.'

Peyton felt uneasy. Did she really want a father who bared his soul to her? 'Maybe Daddy and I can talk later,' she said. 'I just don't feel like I know what to say yet. I was the other way for so long that I don't know what way I need to be now.'

Nora laughed and hugged her. 'I'll relay the message. Do you want to come to church with us, or would you rather just mooch around here and collect yourself?'

'Mooch,' Peyton said gratefully.

Nora went to the door and looked back. 'She did love you, you know,' she said. 'And she loved your father a great deal. What she did had nothing to do with that.'

'How could it not?' Peyton's voice shook.

'They're not at all the same thing,' Nora said. 'Not at all. One is like scratching an itch. When the itch stops, the scratching ends. But the other is better in every way. It lasts. And the other is what she felt for you and your brother and your father. Your father knows that. You will, too, when you're older.'

Peyton heard her father's voice then, calling from the living room. 'You gals ready to go?'

'Let's let this gal sleep in,' Nora called back. 'She had a big day yesterday. She'll have lunch with us. Maybe Howard Johnson's fried clams again. Are you buying?'

'I'll flip you,' he said, and he came into the room.

He sat down on the edge of her bed as Nora had done and lifted her chin with his hand. 'I let you think a terrible thing, and I didn't even know it,' he said. 'We'll have to talk about that. But right now I just want you to know that you are my dearly loved daughter, and my best thing, and that I am very, very proud of you.'

Peyton nodded. She thought hopelessly that if she cried again her throat and nose would finally burst with it.

He leaned forward and hugged her hard and then got up and stood beside Nora. The scent of his pipe and shaving soap lingered.

'Your mother would have loved you totally,' he said. 'It would have been impossible for her not to. I'm telling you the truth about that. Can you be dressed and ready for clams in an hour or so?'

'Yes,' Peyton whispered. 'I can.'

The crystal shell burst, and the world came flooding back in, rude and loud and charged with joy.

8

Peyton went through the next week with the careful deliberation of the newly sighted, carefully putting one foot in front of the other on the earth, not quite trusting it to bear her up, not quite believing that the old blindness would not strike her again. It was not the profound dissociation of the past Sunday, but it was strange enough to keep her preternaturally aware of everything around her, of her own body.

When she looked down she could see her chest, like a shelf. When had that happened? Jeremy Tucker from the tenth grade had run up and kissed her on the cheek at recess. What was she supposed to do about that? Her cheek burned all afternoon.

When Nora came in from her last tutorial that Friday afternoon she found Peyton and Trailways curled up on her bed, record player braying out Brahms.. Peyton was in a tight ball with her eyes closed.

Nora sighed. 'Who stole your bubble gum, toots?' she said, coming across the room to sit beside Peyton.

Peyton opened her eyes. 'I have to make a speech,' she said. 'I have to write it. I have to get up onstage at graduation. It's supposed to be some kind of honour, but I told Mrs Manning I'm not doing it.'

'You could do it wonderfully,' Nora said. 'We could practise it until you weren't frightened any more.'

'I'd die. I'd forget what I was supposed to say. I'd throw up. Everybody would laugh at me. They already think I'm drippy. You know I look like a stork.'

'No,' Nora said. 'I don't know you look like a stork. Haven't you looked at yourself lately? You have a waist and hips and breasts. Your hair is great. You're a pretty girl, Peyton; you have your father's wonderful profile, and his eyes. Lots of girls would kill to look like you.'

'Can you see me leading cheers?' Peyton said bitterly.

'No. But is that really what you want to do? Come on, Peyton. Let's do this thing. Let's work on your speech together. We can practise it. I'll stand in the wings grinning on speech night. We'll get you a knockout new dress.'

'I can't write. What would I write about?'

'I have an idea,' Nora said. 'You know how much you liked the play *Our Town*. What if you did an *Our Town* about Lytton? You could be the Stage Manager and read all the other parts.'

'You mean write about dead people? Nobody wants to hear about dead people at a graduation.'

Nora grinned. 'Dead people don't have to be tragic. You'd make them up to fit what you wanted to say. A young girl like you talking about how sweet it was to be young in Lytton, Georgia. An honoured old man telling about the past here and all the things he witnessed and what he learned over a lifetime. A person who thought Lytton was small potatoes and left, and wandered the wide world, and then came home because there was no place better. You'd talk about the things they remembered—that *you* remember: the long summer twilights, roller-skating in the fall, the town Christmas decorations. Your father would simply burst with pride.'

After a long silence, Peyton said, 'Would you absolutely and positively be there in the wings? Would you help me all the way, and fix the things that are wrong with it?'

'I'll most certainly be there,' Nora said. 'But you're going to have to fix the wrong things yourself. I'm not writing it for you. I'll read it all, though, and I'll rehearse you. You might just surprise yourself by having a good time.'

The next morning Peyton went to the library and checked out *Our Town*. She brought the book home, and she had not read more than two pages before she picked up her pencil and notebook and began to write. She wrote for a long time, and when she looked up it had grown dark and she could hear the voices of Nora and her father out on the front porch, where they sometimes sat after dinner in the soft, fragrant night. She could smell the cool bite of Nora's cigarette, and a sweeter, thicker scent that meant her father was smoking his pipe. The old porch glider creaked, and all at once Peyton was powerfully, giddily happy, and very hungry.

She went out onto the porch. 'Hey,' she said to them.

'Hey, yourself,' her father said. 'Did you just wake up? We saved you some supper.'

'I wasn't asleep,' Peyton said.

Nora looked at her keenly and then reached over and picked up her hand and squeezed it. 'We're off,' she said, grinning.

'Off where?' Frazier said.

'Off to see the Wizard,' Nora said, and she laughed joyously. 'Off our rockers. You just wait and see where we land.'

'I gather I'm not supposed to ask.'

'No. But you'll hear about it soon. Chicken salad in there, Peyton.'

And Peyton went off to eat her late supper and find a way to think about herself that was not, perhaps, so drippy after all.

IT WAS AS IF she had two sets of eyes in those first days of working on the speech. The first set was the one she had had since birth—more educated now, perhaps, focused on her rapidly expanding world, but still her own vision. The other set was somewhere inside her, and it filtered everything through the screen of her writing.

Coming back from Atlanta in the Thunderbird in the late afternoon she would see the Lytton water tank before she saw anything else of the town, and the setting sun would strike the metal into a million facets of glittering colour, and she would think, This is what the person who went away and came back would see first.

She spoke of it to Nora, shyly. 'It's like everything I hear and see and do wants to go into the speech,' she said.

'That's what makes a writer,' Nora said. 'That you see the story in everything. That you go through your life with all your senses open, that you think "what if" a thousand times a day. I knew you'd be good with words, but I didn't know about the seeing. It's not given to many people. It's a gift, Peyton. You can't ever again think of yourself as a loser, as you say. Or even ordinary.'

Peyton's head swam. Pride and fear in equal measure flooded her. And so she went back to her notebook and wrote furiously through the warming afternoons of May. Five weeks. She had only five weeks before graduation.

At night when she came out for supper, she felt as if she were breathing air and seeing lights for the first time. They sat long at the table, talking about their days, and when they finally got up it was to move onto the screened porch and sit in the dark, hearing the ghostly nighttime dissonance of the katydids. Nora and her father almost always lingered when Peyton got up to go to bed. Where once she would have spied on them, now Peyton wrote more in her notebook. But once she went into the living room to ask Nora how to spell something and saw her sitting on the couch watching the soundless television. Her father was stretched out on the sofa with his head in Nora's lap, fast asleep. Nora heard Peyton and looked up and put a finger to her lips.

'Don't wake him. He's had an awful day,' she whispered.

Peyton felt as though she were walking on tiptoe in those days, afraid she might crush something fragile.

She saw Boot one afternoon in the parking lot of the A&P store, where he had taken a job two days a week bagging groceries. He was pushing a full cart, limping along behind a large woman headed for a dirty Pontiac. When Peyton came out of the store with the eggs she had been sent for, he was waiting at the kerb.

'Hey, Peyton,' he said cheerfully.

'Hey, Boot,' she said, sweetness and familiarity flooding over her. She had, she realised, missed Boot enormously.

'Have you seen Ernie?' she asked.

'Don't you know nothin'?' Boot said, swollen with the importance of real news to impart. 'Ernie gone. His mean ol' mama broke her hip and he had to put her in a home up to Hapeville. He sold that little old house and moved in a 'partment to be near her. I think he workin' at McDonald's, like Doreen, only not the same one. He a manager; you know he real smart.'

Ernie in a little paper cap, taking orders from empty-headed teens and fat, blue-rinsed old women who would never in their lifetime know as much as one hundredth of what Ernie's brain held.

Peyton felt tears start. 'Oh, Boot, when?'

'Week and a half ago. It was real sudden. He came by to see me before they left. He working double shifts. That home cost an arm an' a leg, he say.'

'Did he say anything about me?' Peyton whispered.

'Naw. He ain't said nothin' about you since the last time you was at the Losers Club. We shut it down right after that. I miss it, though. It was a lot of fun.'

'I miss it, too,' Peyton said, and she turned away. The tears were streaking down her cheeks now. If Boot saw them he would broadcast it that Peyton McKenzie was crying in the A&P parking lot.

'I'll see you soon, Boot,' she called over her shoulder.

'Yeah,' he called back. 'Tell Mamaw I say hey.'

Peyton did not write in her notebook that afternoon. She lay on her bed and cried and cried, and when the tears finally stopped and she washed her swollen face, she saw for a moment the watery reflection of the pale, pigtailed girl in the too-large blue jeans who used to cut through the undergrowth every afternoon to reach the sanctuary of the Losers Club, and she began to cry again.

'WOW,' NORA SAID, shuffling pages. 'I don't know whether we need an editor or a surgeon.'

They were sitting cross-legged on Nora's bed on a Sunday afternoon, surrounded by drifts of paper. It was thickly hot and airless and Peyton was wearing one of her old sleeveless blouses—too tight across the chest now—and a pair of cutoffs. Nora wore underpants and an enormous, frayed blue oxford-cloth shirt. She was smoking and turning pages intently.

'Now,' Nora said. 'The thing to do first is decide what you want this speech to say.'

'Well . . . just how good it was to live in Lytton years ago, and how everybody sees it differently, but it's still Lytton.'

'Good. Now how would you go about telling that?'

'Through the people who are remembering.'

'OK,' Nora said. 'Let's start with the beginning. Since you're the Stage Manager, what do you want to say?'

'I want to say what the Stage Manager in *Our Town* says.'

'Well, you can't use his exact words, or you'd get sued, but you could say that the play inspired you to think about Lytton and how it must have been long ago, and that you wanted to show people that, because that Lytton won't come again.'

'I want to say exactly that,' Peyton said.

'OK. But it's the only part of it I'm going to write for you. Now let's get into the body of it. I think you could handle maybe three soliloquies. The old woman and the girl are perfect. Whom do you want for your third?'

'The horses,' Peyton said, seeing suddenly the shape of it. 'Their field is on the edge of town, and it would be a way to show Lytton as you came into it back then, and to talk about how it was when people were mainly farmers. And then the young girl, who lived in the middle of town. And then the old woman, because she lived on the other edge of it. It sort of takes you through the town, see?'

'I do indeed.' Nora smiled. 'You ready to start pruning?'

They worked all that afternoon and into the night. When at last they stopped, Peyton was amazed to see that it was nearly midnight. They had culled out the three segments, though.

The next afternoon Nora wrote out the brief introduction, and Peyton read it aloud for the first time: 'More than twenty years ago Thornton Wilder wrote a play called *Our Town*. I went to see it this year in Atlanta, and it made me cry and laugh and wonder. It takes place mainly in the cemetery of a little town, where the dead talk to the Stage Manager, but to me they are as vivid and real as if they were alive. In a sense, they are, through their memories, and I'd like to show you what I think Lytton might have been like through the eyes of some of us who aren't here any more.'

Peyton looked up at Nora, her eyes brimming. 'It's just right,' she said. 'I could never have thought of it.'

Over the next few days the speech took shape and Peyton grew, if not easy, then at least familiar with it. Nora listened and applauded. 'Fabulous,' she said. 'You'll be a sensation.'

And Peyton, flushed with success, began hesitantly to believe her.

Two weeks into their practice sessions, Nora came home and dumped her books loudly on the secretaire and stood rubbing her forehead as if it ached.

'What's the matter?' Peyton said in alarm, coming in from the kitchen.

'Oh, nothing. Just a foul-up at school. I threw a kid out of class and I didn't want to do it, but I didn't have any choice.'

'Was it one of the Negro kids?' Peyton said.

'No. It was one of the cheerleaders,' Nora said.

'You didn't! How wonderful!' Peyton said. 'Which one?'

'Mary Jim Turnipseed. She called one of the black kids a

dimwit, and the child cried in front of the whole class and ran out. Mary Jim started to laugh. I'm afraid I yelled at her.'

'Mary Jim! Lord, Nora, she's the cheerleader captain and homecoming queen. She'll tell her father. He's a judge.'

'I don't care if her father is the lord high executioner. I will not have that kind of thing in my classroom.'

Mary Jim not only told her father about the incident, but also informed her parents that Nora had been teaching them pornography for the last few months, and took home her heavily underlined copy of *The Tropic of Cancer* by way of proof. When her outraged parents asked why she hadn't told them earlier, she said that Miss Findlay had said she'd flunk anybody who told his or her folks. Margaret Turnipseed was on the phone before the words died on Mary Jim's trembling little lips.

They had finished supper and were sitting on the porch talking of the coming summer when the people came. Frazier heard them first, and looked up. There must have been ten or twelve of them, people he had known all his life, neighbours, clients. He did not speak. It was easy to see that they had not come in friendship.

Horace Turnipseed stepped out of the small knot of people and said, 'Frazier, we don't like doing this, but we can't let it go on. Your . . . cousin, or whatever she is, expelled my daughter from her class today. That might not be such a bad thing if Mary Jim deserved it, but she's always been a good girl. I can't imagine what she could have done to warrant that kind of behaviour. But the main thing we can't let pass is what Miss Findlay is teaching our children. I never read anything so dirty. The idea that my child—anybody's child—is reading this stuff is absolutely unacceptable. I'm afraid that we're going to have to ask that you to relieve Miss Findlay of her position.'

'What book are you referring to, Horace?' Frazier asked.

'This.' Horace Turnipseed held up the book. 'This *Tropic of Cancer* thing. There's filth on every page. Every single one.'

'It must have been a real trial for you to have to finish it, Horace,' Peyton's father said. 'Every page, think of it. And it's a big book, too.'

Horace Turnipseed's face reddened. 'Have you ever heard of this book, Frazier?' he said.

'I've read that book,' her father answered. 'I didn't find it in the least offensive. Pretty basic and earthy, but not offensive.'

Peyton goggled. She knew her father had not read the book. She doubted he had even heard of it.

'I will not ask her to resign, Horace,' he said.

There was a shuffling, murmuring silence, and then Aunt Augusta stepped forward into the lamplight.

'Frazier, you are a good man and my brother-in-law,' Augusta McKenzie said. 'But we think perhaps you're . . . too close to this situation. This young woman is a troublemaker. I've said so from the beginning. She is a terrible influence on our young people. How can you subject Peyton to all that? It makes us all wonder in exactly what capacity you keep Miss Findlay in your house.'

Frazier McKenzie stepped forward. He crossed his arms over his chest and looked at his sister-in-law, and then he let his gaze slide over all their faces. Many looked away.

'Miss Findlay is in my house in any capacity she wishes to be,' he said. 'And it is my fondest hope that she will remain so—in any capacity she chooses. It is you who are the troublemaker, Augusta.'

Augusta McKenzie gasped and turned on her heel and clicked rapidly down the path.

Horace Turnipseed cleared his throat. 'Then we have no choice but to go to the whole school board, Frazier,' he said.

'Go,' her father said. Peyton could see that he was trembling.

The small crowd sensed that there was nothing more to say and melted away as silently as it had come. In a moment there was only lamplight and the smell of grass and the sound of crickets.

Her father turned to Nora and took her by the shoulders. 'I meant what I said,' he said. 'I want you with us. We need you. Don't let these idiots run you away. Any capacity, Nora. Any at all.'

Nora's face was as white as a lily in the dimness. 'Don't do this to me, Frazier,' she whispered. 'Don't need me. Don't. I can't carry the weight of it. I can't stay.'

And she wheeled and ran up the stairs to her room.

'Daddy . . .' Peyton said, near tears. 'Daddy, go get her. Don't let her go.'

'I don't think she'll go,' her father said. 'All this business upset her. I don't blame her. She's like a bird. You have to hold her in your open hand. I landed on her too hard tonight.'

'Did you want her to stay . . . you know, like my mother or something?' Peyton could not say, 'Like as your wife.'

'Go to bed, Peyton. We'll straighten it out in the morning.'

But they did not. Nora eluded them like a wild thing. She got up early and stayed late at school. She went often to Atlanta alone and did not ask Peyton and Frazier to go with her. When they did see her, she was noncommittal and pleasant. Her face was pinched and the fire seemed to have gone out of her. She still rehearsed Peyton in her speech, but she did it with the mechanical capability of a paid coach.

Peyton couldn't speak to her of the night on the porch, mostly for fear of what she might hear. But she fretted about her speech. 'You *will* be there, won't you, Nora?' she asked.

'Peyton, you've gotten so good at it that you could do it by yourself,' Nora said. 'But yes, I'll be there. I promised, didn't I?'

The silence in the house spun out. Frazier was once more in his office until all hours. Clothilde trudged heavily about the kitchen. Peyton ached for the Losers Club, at the same time knowing that even if it were still meeting, she had somehow travelled beyond it and could not go back. It was a cold, dull time.

And then Sonny Burkholter came home.

9

Sonny Burkholter was Lytton's claim to fame, its shining star. He had been born to the town's seamstress, a nervous little woman known in Lytton simply as Miss Carrie. They lived for many years in a tiny, neat cottage beside the railroad tracks. There had been a

Mr Burkholter, but he had disappeared, leaving Miss Carrie to bring up Sonny. She idolised him. There was no doubt in her mind that he would touch the world in a very special way.

And he did. After an undistinguished academic career at Lytton High, Sonny cut and ran. For months his frantic mother did not know where he was. Eventually, Sonny surfaced. In a letter to his mother, in which he did not enquire after her well-being, he told her that he was in Los Angeles and had just been cast in a new Western drama as the second lead.

I'm going to come back and build you a house, he wrote. *Watch for me Tuesday night. It's called* Pecos.

Miss Carrie and the whole town watched, and there was no doubt in the collective consciousness that Sonny was going to be a very big television star. Besides his rather ordinary good looks—sharp, diamond-blue eyes, shock of yellow hair, square jaw, chiselled nose—Sonny had something ineffable and immediate on the little screen. The camera loved him. Sonny had only to grin and the set lit up along with the hearts of half of America; when he spoke in his slow drawl sighs were heard from L.A. to Bangor, Maine. He was nineteen years old at the time. The role in the Western was small. But it propelled Sonny into the small-screen stratosphere, and there he had stayed, ending up the season before in a turgid drama called *The Southerners*, in which he played a 'modern Rhett Butler born to raise hell and break hearts'. From the first episode the ratings were off the charts. Raising hell and breaking hearts became, to his adoring public, the very quintessence of southernness. Sonny played it so well that he became a southerner the likes of whom had never trod the red earth of the South.

Speculation about his love affairs was rife and lurid. But Sonny did not settle down. When he came back to Lytton for the first time since he'd left, to install his mother in the mammoth new house he had had built for her just outside town and to speak at the high school, he was unmarried, thirty years old, and richer than Croesus.

Lytton went berserk with pride and joy. There were WELCOME

HOME, SONNY signs all over town, and plans were under way for a parade. But Sonny's publicist sent word that he wanted no special treatment. Sonny was, she said, coming back to find his roots and see his mother into the home they had dreamed about during the years in the cramped little railroad cottage. He would appreciate it if the town would treat him just like anybody else.

It was an inspired public-relations ploy. It let the town worship him for his down-to-earth humility and his devotion to his old mother and laid the groundwork for Sonny to get out of town afterwards as fast as his limousine would take him.

He and Nora collided like meteors. After they met, in the high school cafeteria on Career Day, Sonny decided to stay awhile.

Peyton heard about it from Chloe. Chloe had heard it from her cousin's daughter, who worked in the cafeteria and witnessed the whole thing. As local legend had it, Sonny was escorted to the cafeteria by the tongue-tied president of the student body and the grinning principal. He went through the line 'just like anybody else', and pronounced the lunch the best he had had since he left home.

'There's nothing in the world beats good old-fashioned southern cooking,' he said. This was a stretch, since the school had opted for flaccid grey steaks and uniformly yellow frozen French fries in his honour, but it was widely quoted all the same. He was just getting an Eskimo pie out of the freezer when Nora came into the room.

'She had on that yellow thing that makes her look like a birthday candle,' Chloe reported, 'and somebody had brought her a yellow lily, and she'd stuck it in her hair. That boy walked straight over to her and said, "Will you have lunch with me?" And she said, "Sure." And they sat down together and he ate lunch all over again. They left together, too, in that little pink car.'

Before the day was out, Nora was back with them. Not the coltish Nora who had climbed Peyton's tree in the beginning, not the gleeful Nora who had outraged and overjoyed Lytton in equal parts. And not the languid Nora who had coiled herself on the porch with them in the spring nights. But nevertheless, Nora. The dulled, dimmed stranger of the past few days was gone.

This Nora was not often at home for meals and spent virtually no evenings with Peyton and Frazier. She dashed in and out, hair a brazen banner behind her, green eyes sparkling. She sang in the bathroom and gave Peyton whirlwind hugs on her way out to meet Sonny and paused to kiss Frazier on the cheek and straighten his tie. She seemed to give off sparks. Looking at her, Peyton had the notion that if Nora stuck her finger into a light socket, all the fuses in the house would blow. Despite the hugs and kisses and laughter, there was something about her that was out of control, almost dangerous.

Chloe disliked Sonny Burkholter and was not polite about it.

'He look like an ol' yellow pug dog, with that squished-up nose,' she said after Nora made her watch Sonny's TV programme. 'And he don't act like no southerner I ever seen. Who you seen lately kissin' hands, or tippin' that hat what looks like a lady's?'

'That's a plantation hat.' Nora smiled, refusing to be baited. 'People used to wear them on the big plantations.'

'Ain't no plantation around here I ever seen.'

'Well, you just wait till you see the house Sonny built his mother. It's got everything: columns, oak avenues, horses, everything.'

'She gon' keep slaves?'

'Don't be a butt,' Nora said, and hugged her, and dashed out in a flurry of skirts and petticoats.

The skirts were new. They were not the blazing tropical prints that most of Nora's others were, nor were they willowy, like the rest. They were wide and sprigged with flowers, or made of candy-striped seersucker. And Nora no longer slouched about barefoot.

Peyton had not spent an afternoon or evening in Nora's room since Sonny came home. Pride and pique kept her from begging Nora to rehearse her on the speech, but anxiety about it mounted.

Finally she said, 'Could you possibly listen to my speech tonight? It sounds funny to me and it's only a week away.'

'I can't tonight, kiddo,' Nora said, climbing into a new white dress that drifted around her like a snowbank. 'We're taking Sonny's mother into Atlanta to Emile's. She's never had dinner in Atlanta. Besides, it's time for you to rehearse alone now. You'll be alone when you give it, and you really need to get used to it.'

'But you'll be there . . .'

'Sure, but I can't give the speech for you. Now's as good a time as any to start standing alone. You can do it.'

No, I can't, Peyton thought. She was suddenly very angry at her cousin. This was to have been her special time with Nora, but Nora had given it all to Sonny without a backward glance.

'You're going to look pretty silly, all of you jammed into that little car,' Peyton said.

'We're taking Sonny's limo. He hates to use it, but with his mother he has to, and besides, his driver is dying of boredom.'

Peyton could not leave it alone. 'I'd have thought a big TV star could drive his own car,' she said. 'Can't he drive?'

Nora shot her a look. 'Of course he can, but he doesn't like to drive the limo around here. He thinks it looks ostentatious. Knock it off about Sonny, Peyton. He's a nice guy. You'll see when you meet him.'

'I don't want to meet him.'

'Well, then, you can sit in your room all night, because I've invited him to dinner.'

'Daddy's just going to love that. Did you ask him?'

'Yes. He said he'd be honoured, and by all means to ask him.'

Peyton thought of the night on the porch when her father had taken hold of Nora's shoulders and said, 'I meant what I said. I want you to stay. I want you with us. We need you . . . Any capacity, Nora. Any at all.' She remembered his face as he said it. He had looked younger by far than she had ever seen him. He had looked happy. He did not look young now, or happy.

'I bet he didn't mean it,' she said to Nora.

'Well, if he didn't he'll never let me know about it, because he's a gentleman, and the kindest man I've ever met.'

Then why isn't that enough? Peyton said in her head. Her heart hurt as if someone had hit her in the chest.

She ploughed on with her rehearsing. At first the space where Nora was not swallowed her voice and her will, but after a few days she saw that, given no mishaps, she could probably read the speech competently. The magic and music had gone from it, though. But with Nora there in the wings, perhaps the magic would come back.

The judge and his coterie were as good as their word. Nora was dismissed only days after the confrontation on the front steps. She never spoke of it, did not seem to remember that she had had a job. She lived entirely in the wake of Sonny Burkholter.

Her father did not, this time, shut Peyton out or pull away from her. He spent his nights with her on the porch or in front of the TV, and he never missed breakfast or dinner with her, and she could tell he was trying to enter her world. He asked about her days and hugged her frequently, and made a small game of her graduation speech.

'Still not going to tell me?'

'No.'

'I know. You're giving it in Japanese.'

'You're silly.'

'Then you're going to tap dance while you're speaking.'

'*Daddy . . .*'

But she laughed. They both laughed. If they laughed enough, Peyton could not hear the emptiness where Nora's rich laugh should be. Once it would have been enough just to be this close to Daddy, she thought bleakly. Almost, it was.

She was still angry with Nora, and not the least of her anger was for her father. Nora had to know that Frazier wanted her to stay, she thought. If she wasn't going to be with us like she'd always been, she should have moved out so we wouldn't have to watch her carry on with that jerk.

Sonny came to dinner the week of graduation. Nora had asked for a completely southern meal and had presented Chloe with the menu: fried chicken, turnip greens with cornmeal dumplings, fresh corn, sliced tomatoes, biscuits, and chicken gravy. And peach cobbler for dessert. These were all the things Sonny pined for out in California, she said.

'They ain't got chicken in California?' Clothilde had grumped.

'Nobody in California fries anything, Chloe, and they've never heard of turnip greens.'

Promptly at six o'clock the long black limousine slid up the kerb in front of the house and Sonny got out of the back seat—or one of the back seats, Peyton thought. She was watching from the screened porch, behind a big fern.

Sonny came up the steps and Nora stood in the doorway to greet him. She wore yellow pique and he wore a bursting blue T-shirt, white trousers, and black sunglasses. She took him by the hand and led him onto the porch.

'Frazier, this is Sonny,' she announced. 'He's heard all about you. He said he was almost afraid to meet you. Sonny, this is my Cousin Frazier McKenzie.'

'We're pleased to have you,' Frazier said, standing up and putting out his hand to Sonny. 'We've seen a lot of you on TV.'

'The pleasure is mine, sir,' Sonny said. He took Frazier's hand in both his own and pressed it, and looked into his eyes.

'Needless to say, you're all Nora talks about,' he told Frazier. 'You and Miss Peyton here.' He smiled over at Peyton behind her fern. His teeth were blinding white and his voice was small and high, as if he had a bee trapped in his jaws. They must do something on TV to make it sound lower, Peyton thought. She was so delighted with his voice that she came out from behind the fern and let him take her hand and bow over it and kiss it. She looked up at Nora to see if she was successfully concealing her laughter, but Nora was not laughing. She was smiling tenderly upon Sonny.

'Didn't I tell you they were special?' she said.

It was an awful dinner; Peyton felt as if it went on for aeons. Sonny did most of the talking. He began the moment they sat down.

The table was set with pink linen and flowers, and her mother's silver candlesticks held pale pink candles. When Chloe came in with their plates, Sonny rolled his blue eyes and mimicked a swoon. When she had left again, he turned to Frazier and said, 'It's what I've missed most, this good old-fashioned southern cooking. And nobody does it like these good old Negro mammies, do they? You be good to her; she's worth her weight in gold.'

At first Peyton thought she had not heard correctly. Then she looked at her father. He was looking down at his plate with interest.

She looked at Nora. Surely she would demolish him with the cold knife of her tongue. 'Mammies' indeed!

But Nora merely said, 'She's the best cook I've ever known.'

From then on Sonny talked of Hollywood and the show; he tossed out words and phrases like 'production schedule' and 'ratings' and 'syndication'. Her father looked gravely interested. Nora looked as if she were hearing an Ave Maria.

What is *wrong* with her? Peyton thought. He's a jerk.

That night before she fell asleep, Peyton prayed: 'Please, God, don't let her go off with him. Please don't let her leave.'

The day after the dinner Sonny flew to New York for a few days and Nora was back in spirit as well as in flesh. It was as if she had never been away. No one remarked about it; they simply slid into their old life as if they were sliding into warm water.

On one of the days they went into Atlanta, and Frazier did some business at the courthouse while Nora and Peyton shopped. Nora had trimmed Peyton's hair and it was back in its lustrous tousle, and they found, at Rich's, an ivory polished-cotton sheath with a standaway collar that made Peyton look, as Nora said, like a lighted candle. Even Peyton could see that it was an extraordinary dress. In it, a person could do anything, even make a speech on the stage of Lytton Grammar School. Nora bought it for her.

They drove home in the late afternoon, singing at the top of their lungs. Oh, yes, Nora was back.

'Do you think she's trying to say she's sorry about taking up with that jerk?' Peyton asked her father that night when he came in to tuck her in. He'd been doing that every night, and after the first embarrassed stiffness, both of them had enjoyed the ritual.

He was silent for a moment, and then he sat down on the edge of her bed. 'No, I don't,' he said, looking at her. 'I think she's saying goodbye.'

'No,' Peyton cried. It came out as involuntarily as breath.

'You know she never said she'd stay,' he said, smoothing the hair off her face.

'But she wanted to, I know she did . . . she always talked about how safe she felt here, and how she just wanted to be with us.'

'She needs to be able to do what's right for her,' Frazier said. 'We can't hold her if she wants to go.'

'Do . . . you want her to stay?'

He smiled. 'Let it be, Peyton. Be happy that she's happy.'

'I bet she's not. I bet it's just his stupid money. She'd hate living in Hollywood. Can you see her out there?'

'Yes,' he said. 'I can.'

On Thursday of that week Nora listened to a last run-through of the speech Peyton would give the next night. Peyton dressed for it in the ivory dress Nora had bought her, and her mother's pearls.

'That was perfect,' Nora said. 'And look at you. I'm going to have to hog-tie Sonny; he'll try to make a play for you for sure.'

'Is he coming?'

'Yes. He wouldn't miss it for the world. He's coming back tomorrow afternoon. I'm going to meet him at the airport and we're coming straight to the auditorium. It's practically his last night before he has to go back to California, so you should be honoured.'

'Are you going with him?' Peyton said, elaborately examining her hemline in the mirror.

'He hasn't asked me,' Nora said. 'But if he does, you'll be the first to know. Of course, it certainly wouldn't mean I'd go . . .'

'He's rich. You'd never have to worry about money again.'

'I don't worry about it now. That's not worthy of you, Peyton. Let's drop this right now.' Her tone was chilly. As she left the room, Peyton took a last look at her reflection in the mirror. The candle's flame had gone out.

NORA WAS NOT THERE the next morning.

'She gone to Atlanta to do a little shopping,' Chloe said.

Peyton pushed away her plate. Her head felt light and her ears buzzed. Why had Nora left her on this morning? She didn't have to leave for the airport until late in the day.

Nora was not back in the afternoon, either. Peyton stayed in her room and looked at her watch a hundred times. Finally she knew that Nora would be on her way to the airport to retrieve Sonny and that she would not see her now until that night in the wings.

When she had dressed and sat down to put on her make-up the way Nora had taught her, her hands shook so that she could manage only clownish red spots on her cheeks and a crazy slash of lipstick. She washed it all off.

'You look beautiful,' her father said as they got into the car to go to the school.

Those honoured sat in tiered rows on the stage, on benches borrowed from the gymnasium. The school choir sat in chairs just below them. It was very hot. Peyton felt lightheaded and removed, stricken with terror.

Nora . . . Peyton slid a look at the wings. She saw the drama coach, but no Nora. But she had thirty minutes yet . . .

They had the prayer. The principal stood up and welcomed everyone. The audience rustled and fanned.

Peyton heard the principal telling the audience that the valedictory address would be given by Miss Peyton McKenzie, and that he was sure they were all eager to hear what she had to say.

Nora did not come.

Peyton stood up and walked to the lectern. Her hands were so wet that they left prints on the pages of her speech. She looked out into the audience and could see nothing but the haze of lights.

Nora did not come.

'More than twenty years ago Thornton Wilder wrote a play called *Our Town,*' she whispered. Her voice shook.

'Louder,' the drama coach hissed from the wings.

Peyton ploughed ahead. She finished the introduction and started into the segment about the horses.

'We are horses,' she faltered. 'Let us tell you how it was then, on the farms of Lytton, Georgia . . . .'

From the audience there was a muffled whinny, and a patter of smothered laughter. Peyton's hands and lips numbed. She read on. Nora was not there. Peyton would have felt her if she had been.

'We were happy here,' she finished up. 'We were fed and groomed with love, and nobody ever beat us in our lives.'

'You can't beat a dead horse,' a voice in the audience said. This time the laughter was not muffled.

Nora did not come.

Sickened and dizzy, Peyton started into the segment about the young girl. She knew she was whispering. She did not care.

'My name is Elizabeth,' she quavered. 'I was sixteen years old when I died, and I loved my life. There were no streetlights in my Lytton, but there were gas lamps, and I used to walk in their soft light in the spring nights, smelling the honeysuckle and mimosa, laughing with my friend, all dressed up. We did not always know where we were going, but it did not matter. Sometimes we just went to the little meadow behind the bandstand and lay in the cool grass.'

'Must have been a real good friend,' someone called.

'Yeah,' another boy yelled. 'I've had a lay behind that bandstand, too. I never knew you could die of it, though.'

There was an airless hush, and then the auditorium exploded into laughter. Peyton saw her father stand up and turn and glare at the audience, saw him hold up his hands for quiet. The laughter spiralled up.

Peyton turned and walked off the stage. She did not turn her head right or left as she went through the wings.

The drama coach put out her hand. 'Peyton, honey,' she said. 'It wasn't you. It was those idiot boys.'

In the schoolyard Peyton broke into a trot. By the time she was a block from home she had taken off her shoes and tossed them into the grass beside the sidewalk and was running flat out. Her stockings were shredded, and the cement of the sidewalk abraded her feet. She did not feel it. She felt nothing but a simple need to be in the tree house. In the dark.

Where Nora was not.

Without hesitation she went up her tree and huddled on the floor of the tree house. It felt cramped, too small, a toy. She knew she would not come here again.

She laid her head on her crossed arms and sank down into the leafy darkness of the tree branches. She waited.

In what seemed like an eyeblink she heard her father's voice under her tree. 'Come on down, honey,' he said. 'Come on down and let's go in and have some hot chocolate. It's not the end of the world, and it's not your fault. Those boys will be punished.'

Peyton burrowed her head deeper into her arms.

'Peyton, come down from there,' Aunt Augusta's voice shrilled.

She did not reply.

'Peyton, I can't just leave you up there,' her father said pleadingly. 'Please don't make me come up and get you.'

'Let me get her,' Nora's voice said. 'I did it once before. She'll come down for me, and we can talk this business out.'

Peyton lifted her head and looked down. Nora stood at the foot of the tree, hands on hips, looking up. She had on the yellow dress, and she shone in the darkness like foxfire. She was smiling. Beyond her, at the kerb, stood the little pink car; she and Sonny must have come home and Peyton had not heard. Sonny stood beside Nora, looking serious and concerned.

'I apologise, kiddo,' Nora said. 'We got hung up and couldn't get back. Listen, you don't care about those cretins. They think the backs of cigarette packs are literature. I'm just going to come up now. That's how we met, remember?'

She put her hands on the lower limbs of the tree to swing herself up. The yellow skirt belled out around her.

Peyton was on her feet before she even knew she was rising. She leaned far out over the railing of the tree house. 'Don't you come up here!' she screamed. 'Don't you dare come up here! What makes you think you can just come up here and take care of me, like nothing even happened? *You told me you'd be there and you weren't!* You can't take care of anybody! You can't even take care of your own baby!'

The silence was absolute. In it Peyton could hear the katydids start up, and her own blood thundering in her ears.

'Did you all know that Nora has a little boy?' she called down, in a voice of such ugly gaiety that it hurt even her ears. 'He's five years old and his name is Roberto and he lives in Cuba with his grandmother because Nora went off and left him. He's black, and his father is black, and he was never Nora's husband . . .'

A blindness was roaring down on her, but through it she

thought she saw her father's face go still and blank, and saw Sonny Burkholter's slight recoiling, and heard Aunt Augusta's gasp. Nora said nothing; her face did not change. Then she turned and walked towards the house. She did not look back. The others did not move.

'Go tell the Devil!' Peyton screamed after her, leaning further out still. 'Go tell the Devil!'

The sodden railing gave, and Peyton followed her rage and anguish down into darkness.

IT WAS AS IF SHE lived and moved and slept in deep green water. It seemed like an eternity after she broke free of it, but her father said that it had been only three days.

'You have a doozy of a thing called a cranial haematoma,' he said. 'It knocked you out for three days. But you're fine now, and there won't be any aftereffects as long as you stay quiet. You've got a broken collarbone, too. And a couple of cracked ribs.'

Peyton remembered, dimly, about the night of the graduation and the tree, but she did not let her memory take her any further.

When she came home from the hospital she asked to be in the upstairs bedroom. Nora's room.

'You sure?' her father said.

'Yes. The other one's too small. And Trailways won't stay in any room but this one.'

So it became Peyton's room, with nothing left in it of her Cousin Nora. Peyton floated on pain medication, and slept and woke and watched the little television her father had brought her, and ate the meals Chloe brought, and stroked Trailways, and never thought of the room's last occupant except once or twice when she thought, in that place between sleep and waking, that she smelt Nora's perfume.

June seeped away, and July came, hot and still. Peyton did not ask about Nora. She did not ask about Sonny. She did not care.

On a still, hot day in the third week of July, Peyton finally looked into the mirror. A bleached, yellowed skull looked back, with shapeless, lank hair on one side of its head and stubble over white scalp on the other. There was a long, welted red scar in the stubble.

'I need a haircut,' she said, and then she realised that there would be no haircut because Nora was gone. She began to cry, and she cried, on and off, through the afternoon and most of the night. Her father lay on her bed beside her, holding her face to his shoulder. Grey light was just showing under her venetian blinds when she stopped.

'You better now?' her father said.

'I don't know,' she said. 'Daddy, do you pray?'

'Yes, I do.'

'Does it always feel to you like God is listening?'

'I don't always feel Him, but I think He does listen. Most of the time, anyway.'

'What good does it do if He's not listening all the time?'

'I think He wants us to handle what we can on our own. Why do you want to know?'

'Because I prayed for Nora to stay, and she might have, but then I ran her away myself. I thought maybe I'd done it wrong.' And she began to cry again. 'I hate Nora,' she sobbed. 'She ruined my life!'

'Well, you didn't do such a bad job of ruining hers,' he said.

'What do you mean?'

'I mean old Sonny was gone before you hit the ground.'

'When did Nora go?'

'I'm not sure. She was gone when I came home from the hospital the next morning.'

'She didn't even care whether I was badly hurt or not.'

'She did. She called from Alabama late that day to see about you. We knew then that you'd be all right. Chloe told her.'

'Have you talked to her?'

'No.'

'When you said . . . that Sonny was gone, you mean gone back to Hollywood, without her?'

'Precisely. I think he hit the road before daylight.'

'I don't understand.'

'How would it look if the new Rhett Butler was keeping company with a lady who had a black baby out of wedlock?' her father said. Incredibly, there was laughter in his voice.

Peyton smiled tentatively, and then she began to laugh, too.

'Rat Butler,' she said, and collapsed against him in laughter.

Presently she stopped. 'So you know where she is?'

'Texas,' he said. 'I had a letter the day before yesterday. She's working in a library there. She says it's a funny little town but it doesn't hold a candle to Lytton.'

Peyton felt fresh pain flooding her. She closed her eyes against it. Nora, in a dusty little town in Texas, working in a library . . .

'What about the car?'

'She sold the car. She said she didn't like it any more. She has a Plymouth now.'

Peyton shook her head back and forth, grinding her face into her father's shoulder. 'I loved that car,' she said.

'There was a message for you in the letter,' he said. 'I've been carrying it around for days, waiting for you to want to hear it.'

He pulled a much-folded sheet of stationery from his shirt pocket. Peyton closed her eyes and waited.

'"Tell Peyton it wasn't her fault. If I know her, she'll carry around a wagonload of guilt for the rest of her life if somebody doesn't take it away from her. But it was all me. Tell her it's what I do best, run. I've been doing it all my life. I preach freedom and spontaneity; I know better than anybody in the world how to draw people out and get them to trust me. It's one of the only talents that were given to me. And when I have them hanging on to me, I run. I leave them twisting in the wind. The truth is that I'm dying for safety, and a place to be, but I can't stand it when somebody offers it to me. I punish the people who open themselves to me. Tell her that she was born with the gift of a constant heart, and that's worth a hundred of me. Tell her to stop feeling guilty and start writing, and that she did me a favour. Ol' Sonny is nothing but a redneck with money, and he'll be a real hog when he's forty. I knew that even when I was following him around like a puppy dog. He was my ticket away from the love and trust you both offered me. I deserved him, but I'm mighty glad to be rid of him. Tell Peyton I love her, just as I do you."'

It was signed, simply, 'Nora.'

'What does that mean?' Peyton said.

'I think it means that you grew up and Nora didn't.'

Peyton's heart cracked. Nora stood before her whole and living and vivid, laughing. Peyton could count every copper freckle. Loss drowned her.

'I hate her,' she said, weeping, but she said it doubtfully. Surely hate did not hurt like this.

'Well,' her father said, 'you'd just as soon hate a butterfly. We didn't give one single thought to what *she* might need. We just climbed up on her wings. We loved it there; it was a wonderful ride. And she tried to hold us up, but we were too heavy. Finally she had to drop us and go. All the time she wanted an anchor, a place to light, and we were too busy riding her wings to see that.'

'She said I'd always be safe with her. She *said* that!'

Her father put his chin down on her head and began to rock her like a child. 'Nobody's safe, Peyton, and nobody's free,' he said. 'There's only somewhere between safe and free, and what people are. We all try so hard to be strong, or free, or safe, or whatever it is we think we need most . . . and in the end all we can ever be is just us. And it's enough because it has to be. There's not anything else.'

'I don't know how to do that. I'm not even sure who me is.'

'Well, this is what we do,' he said. 'We try to give what little we have to somebody who hasn't got it, and maybe they try to give us back some of what they have that we haven't got. That's what love is. That's all it is. You can do that. You already do it.'

They were silent awhile. Then he said, 'We both still need Nora, I guess.'

'No. We don't.'

'Yes. For one thing, you need a haircut.' He smoothed her hair back from her forehead. 'Let's go get her,' he said.

'Are you *crazy?* Go get her? After what she did to you?'

'Yep. You and me and even Trailways if he'll behave himself. Drive to New Orleans and then on over to Texas.'

Peyton saw it in her mind, the empty, heat-shimmering roads.

Small diners and gas stations and neon cactuses. Hamburgers and milkshakes in the car at McDonald's and Burger King.

'When would we go?'

'Now. This afternoon.'

'She wouldn't come,' Peyton whispered. 'Not after what I did . . .'

'Bet she would. She needs us, too. She really does. I should have seen that sooner.'

'What if she doesn't think so?'

He grinned suddenly. 'Then we'll pester her until she changes her mind,' he said. 'We'll plonk our guitars under her window and yowl like a couple of tomcats until she gives up. She'll come.'

Peyton began to laugh. She ran to the window and jerked the clattering blinds up. Red-gold light smote her. Joy took her then, and hurled her, still laughing, out into the brightening day.

ANNE RIVERS SIDDONS

With fifteen novels to her name and fourteen million copies of her books in print, Anne Rivers Siddons is firmly established as one of America's top-selling authors. Her work is often described as 'women's fiction', a label she doesn't like because to her it suggests 'romances and light, fluffy things'. Her novels, as *Nora, Nora* illustrates, have more to them than that.

Nora, Nora, like many of Anne Rivers Siddons's books, is set in America's Deep South. It takes place in the early Sixties, a time when civil rights battles were raging, especially in cities like Atlanta, not far from the small town where Siddons grew up. As a student she wrote a column for her university's newspaper in support of racial integration and was asked by the dean of students if she would perhaps like to reconsider her views. She refused. 'I was really aware of the disapproval, and I got a first taste of how it might feel to espouse a cause that was not everybody else's,' she says, recalling those times.

Siddons, who now lives in Charleston, North Carolina, explains how she came to create the character of Nora, the flamboyant cousin who blazes into the life of twelve-year-old Peyton and helps the girl through the painful process of growing up. 'There's a good bit of Peyton in me,' she says. 'I had two loving parents, but I was an only child in a household of books with no neighbours around and a feeling of being alone. Nora is the worldly-wise big sister I wish I'd had—brave, funny, loving, devoted to me. Someone who would show me how to grow up and live in the world.'

201-008